Chrysalis

Also by
John D. Lambert

The Intersections Romance Series

Available Now:
Divergent

Coming Soon:
Toast
Resonance

Also Available Now

Crimson Leaves: Poetry Celebrating Romance

Bask in the glow of love with *Crimson Leaves*, where every page whispers the language of romance.

Celebrate romance with the finest ancient, old, and contemporary love poetry from great poets worldwide, featuring:

- Over 200 love poems, timeless and new
- Heartfelt quotations and meditations
- Passionate letters and lyrics
- And introducing Poetic Hugs & Kisses™

Chrysalis

Book 2 in the
Intersections Romance Series

JOHN D. LAMBERT

RESOURCE *Publications* • Eugene, Oregon

CHRYSALIS

Copyright © 2026 John D. Lambert. All rights reserved. Except for brief quotations in critical publications or reviews, no part of this book may be reproduced in any manner without prior written permission from the publisher. Write: Permissions, Wipf and Stock Publishers, 199 W. 8th Ave., Suite 3, Eugene, OR 97401.

Resource Publications
An Imprint of Wipf and Stock Publishers
199 W. 8th Ave., Suite 3
Eugene, OR 97401

www.wipfandstock.com

PAPERBACK ISBN: 979-8-3852-7994-4
HARDCOVER ISBN: 979-8-3852-7995-1
EBOOK ISBN: 979-8-3852-7996-8

VERSION NUMBER 05/27/26

Contents

Chrysalis: A transformative period where a hidden or evolving self emerges from a protective outer shell, replacing old self-perceptions with a more integrated sense of identity and personal worth.

Another word for chrysalis is aurelia,
from the Latin word for gold: Aurum.

Preface

Chrysalis is an intersex story that includes romance, not the other way around. The romance has to wait in this case—but when it comes, it's worth the wait.

At least one out of every 5,500 people is intersex—biologically part male and part female. With a U.S. population of 350 million, there are at least 62,000 Americans who are intersex.

If a few similar conditions are included, the estimates are far higher, but most of them don't know it because their symptoms are too mild to notice. This is a story about one of them who has a dramatic discovery.

Chrysalis is a first-person POV short novel from the perspective of someone with ovotesticular syndrome, as they become aware of their condition, begin learning to live with it, and uncover what it means to their prospects for romance.

Manhattan Talent

Henry and Mike were laughing like hyenas in the breakroom when I trudged in, and Henry safid, "Leo! You oughta do this!"

Mike kept laughing as Henry toned it down a notch to talk to me. "Seriously, Leo, you're the best looking guy here! If any of us have a shot at using this to get out of here, it's you!"

I wasn't interested in being the butt of a joke, but the idea of getting out of telephone technical support hooked me. "Yeah?"

"Yeah, yeah!" he said, showing me his phone. "This company's looking for models, men and women. All you have to be is good-looking. High pay, all training provided, no experience necessary!

"They're trying to crowdsource auditions to find new talent, and all you have to do is download their app, submit your photo, and boom—the app tells you if they might be interested in you."

In between bouts of laughter, Mike said, "Henry tried it, and it was an instant rejection!"

"Their loss," Henry confirmed with a grin.

They teased me some more while yakking and laughing, but their break was over so they had to quit.

"It's Manhattan Talent," Henry said on his way out. "Seriously, you should try it!"

I got a cup of black coffee and sat down with my back to a wall, as usual, so no one could see my phone over my shoulder. I sighed deeply and tried to relax my shoulders as I turned my phone on while wishing once again that we were allowed to play handheld game machines while on break.

With no one else on break and nothing more important to browse, I did a search for Manhattan Talent and looked for third-party info first.

I didn't see any scam reports—only good reviews. They're a private modeling and talent agency, known mostly for their fashion industry work, located here in New York City, which makes sense for a talent agency, I guessed.

So I went to their website, which looked legit, and it made it clear all auditions had to start with their app, but it mentioned you could download the app and audition both free and anonymously. Which also made sense, because I doubted Henry would've paid to do that.

I downloaded the app, opened it, and it hyped what a great opportunity they were offering and how easy it was to audition.

Fashion, acting, and other opportunities . . . high pay, international travel possible, all expenses paid, no experience required, all training provided . . . oh, and this was important, "Manhattan Talent will never ask you for money. Never. Not for fees, not for headshots, not for anything."

To audition . . . take a photo of your face from the front and from the side. Hair doesn't matter as long as it doesn't cover the face or ears. Age . . . Height . . . Weight . . . Oh, interesting . . . "Sex: Male, Female, or Intersex. Huh."

"The Manhattan Talent system will promptly tell you if you have a look that we're looking for. Additional information provided to those who pass this audition."

I set my phone face down and thought about it as I continued to nurse my coffee. High pay, no experience required.

They probably get thousands of people doing this, and the more people auditioning, the lower the chances of any one person, like me. And if their system was decent, they should be able to handle millions of auditions. But . . . auditioning was easy, free, and anonymous . . .

My phone had the app open, and it'd only take a few seconds to snap a couple of pictures . . . but if someone came into the breakroom right at that moment . . . nope, nope, nope.

A few hours later I got home to the tiny apartment where I rented a tiny room. No one else was home, and I fixed myself something to eat and enjoyed it in peace for once.

After cleaning up after myself, I went to my room, closed the door, propped up on my pillows on the bed and got my phone out to while away some time.

After keying in my security login PIN, my phone opened to the Manhattan Talent app, which I'd forgotten about. I started to close it, but changed my mind, and figured I'd waste a minute or two to try it.

Twenty-two years old, five-foot-seven, 125 pounds, male, photo from the front . . . photo from the side . . . and . . . submit.

"Congratulations! You're one of the very few who pass the Manhattan Talent photo audition!"

Huh. I'd be thinking it's a scam, except Henry got rejected . . . Well, now what do they say . . .

Next step is . . . oh, I have to drop the anonymity and schedule an interview. I guess that makes sense. Name, address, phone . . .

Hey! They'll pay me a hundred bucks for completing the enrollment info, another hundred for doing the interview, and five hundred if I pass the interview! Dang!

Let's see . . . payment methods . . . yeah, they include one I already use, and even offer a crypto option . . . that's cool—or would be if I set up a crypto wallet.

I put my personal information in and moments later got a notification on my money app. A hundred bucks. For nothing. That was . . . impressive, somehow.

And two notifications in the app . . . one about the payment . . . oh, wow, and they say since I live in New York City they'll send a limo to take me to my interview! Me? In a limo?!

And I can schedule a two-hour interview any weekday, from 10 a.m. to 2 p.m. Since Thursday's my usual day off, I won't have to miss work . . .

But no more info about the whole deal. I guess that will come after the interview, if I pass. I wonder what the pass/fail rate is for these interviews?

The interview schedule had an opening on my next day off in three days—this Thursday, at 10, so I took that, and a minute later a notification said the limo would pick me up at 9 a.m.

I had a hundred questions, but there wasn't any other interesting information in the app, and there wasn't a way to contact them.

I searched the Internet, and found tons about the company, but the only posts I found about this auditioning process were from people who didn't pass it . . . and the only contact info I could find was their street address and phone numbers for some very business sounding offices.

With nothing else to learn until the interview, I put my phone down on my bed and thought all this over.

It was exciting . . . it might mean a much more enjoyable and much better paying job . . . but it'd be better not to get my hopes up yet. Try to hold that off at least until I saw how the interview went.

After a while, I went back to my usual evening activities of doom scrolling on my old, cheap Android phone with a cracked screen and playing my one luxury—my treasured handheld game machine.

Except all this Manhattan Talent business kept distracting me.

Should I tell anyone about this? If I tell my roommates or coworkers, they might tease me if I don't pass the interview . . .

Come to think of it, they'd probably start teasing me immediately.

Except Henry. And I only started this because he urged me to. But if I told him, would he blab it to others? Better to wait and see what happened after the interview.

What would happen after the interview? If I didn't pass, nothing, I guess. Just something else to try to forget.

And if I pass? Manhattan Talent lists fashion, movies, TV, and theater as their areas. They wouldn't want a guy for fashion—I don't think—and the others are all acting.

So . . . if I pass . . . they might start training me to become an actor?

Was I good-looking enough for that? Well, I passed the first photo-based audition, so . . . maybe? But probably not as a leading man, because those tend to be tall, with very few exceptions.

Supporting actor . . . I wonder how much that paid? Not the biggest bucks, but more than tech support?

Hmm . . . maybe I'd have to keep doing tech support and do acting on the side?

That thought was a huge let-down.

Well, they already paid me a hundred bucks, and I'd get at least another hundred. And if I passed this interview, another five hundred, even if I never did anything else.

Seven hundred total, for nothing!

I never had much growing up, and ever since I got a job, I'd been scrimping and living as cheaply as possible to save every penny I could, and so far I only had a little over twelve hundred bucks. Seven hundred was two or three years' worth of painful saving.

I went to the bathroom and studied my face in the mirror. Same old face . . . but a new realization.

Maybe I was "good" looking—Henry genuinely seemed to think so, but I certainly wasn't rugged-looking. What kind of characters would someone with my face play?

I couldn't come up with an answer for that, but maybe I'd find out in the interview.

Sleep didn't come easily that night, which made working the next day even worse than usual.

And the trip home from work the next day was weird. I was excited, but trying not to be. One more day of work, and then my interview. And the limo ride!

That evening was worse than the first one. Lots more questions, and not a single answer.

For the second night in a row, I didn't sleep well, and the next day at work was hell.

On the way home, my mind was kind of numb from lack of sleep, but at least my interview was the next morning.

Except . . . if I couldn't sleep again, I'd be a zombie and fail.

To my surprise, I went to sleep quickly that night, and slept well. Due to exhaustion, I guess, but at least the timing was good.

I even woke up happy, which almost never happened. Probably because I was about to ride in a limo and get paid a hundred dollars for showing up.

Even if I failed the interview completely, I'd still be two hundred dollars better off than I'd been before Henry urged me to check this out.

Interview

Once in the limo, I asked the driver what he could tell me about Manhattan Talent, but he said he knew nothing about them—just who to pick up, where, and where to drop me off. He didn't even know if he'd be the driver taking me home.

I wore my only white shirt with my only tie, my best khaki slacks, and my very old but rarely used thrift store dress shoes.

The entrance to the office tower was impressive, and so was the lobby. Manhattan Talent was on the eighteenth floor.

When I got off the elevator, along with two other people, there were lots of people going through the area in front of the elevators, but it wasn't a hallway—it was a big open area, and there was a long reception counter straight ahead. That meant Manhattan Talent took up the whole floor!

I made my way over and gave one of the women my name, and she looked me up, smiled, and asked me to follow her. She took me to a room that was spacious, but only had a small table and six chairs.

"Mrs. Forth will be right with you. Would you like anything to drink?"

The idea of throwing up due to nervousness crossed my mind. "No, thank you."

The receptionist left, and only a couple of minutes later, a kind of middle-aged executive-looking woman entered.

"Leo? I'm Sylvia Forth," she said with a smile. "I'm here to start your interview. Would you like something to drink?"

"No, thank you."

She sat down, fiddled with her phone for a moment, set it down, and then looked me over. It felt a little awkward, but I didn't say anything because I didn't think of anything worth saying yet.

My phone dinged—I'd forgotten to silence it.

"Check your phone, Leo."

I did. A notification of a deposit of one hundred dollars.

"Um . . . thank you very much," I managed to say.

"Thank you for coming," Mrs. Forth replied.

"We've been finding high quality models and actors a long time, and we've been very successful. We still rely on our older methods, but the AI has made us even better.

"In addition to searching for new models and actors, we also keep an eye out for the very few individuals who have certain characteristics regarding something else. You fit the criteria for that additional reason, as judged by our AI—which has a remarkable track record so far."

She paused, but I didn't reply. I wanted to know what the additional reason was, but I expected her to tell me without me having to ask.

"You have an ectomorph body type, which is at least partly why you're thin and find it very difficult to build muscles."

I could feel my face flushing in embarrassment, because she was right, but so what? Lots of guys weren't muscular.

She had tapped something on her phone and a computer screen lit up on the wall behind her, but to the side, so I could see clearly . . . a picture of a strikingly beautiful young woman.

Okay . . . but what was the point of that? I glanced back at Mrs. Forth, and she seemed to be studying me again, more intently this time.

She tapped her phone again, and the front-face photo I submitted was side-by-side with the beautiful woman.

And I realized the beautiful woman was . . . *me?* Me with long hair and makeup. I felt *very* confused . . .

Moments later, Mrs. Forth tapped her phone again. The makeup layer disappeared, and both pictures were identical except for hair length.

"This is an AI enhancement of your photo, Leo. And all it did was lengthen your hair and add makeup. That's all."

I don't know how long we were both quiet, but my mind was reeling, and I couldn't stop looking at the photos.

One was me. One was me with long hair and makeup. But two very different people.

Mrs. Forth turned the makeup layer on the AI image off and on a few times. It was definitely my picture under the makeup.

"Okay . . ." I finally managed to say. "I never . . . saw myself like this before . . . I don't know what to think . . ."

"Our AI judged your facial features and your neck as highly feminine . . . and—"

She kept talking, but I lost track of what she was saying.

Highly feminine. Me? Highly feminine?

I tuned in again.

"We get very few people in this situation, Leo, but of those we do, most of them aren't totally surprised by this. Have you really never noticed your feminine traits before?"

My face felt hot. All I could do was stare at the girl on screen and shake my head to reply.

"Leo, look at me."

I did.

"You're a good-looking guy," she said, "but you're a drop-dead gorgeous woman."

I shifted my gaze back to the AI image . . . of me.

I didn't know how to feel.
I'm not sure I felt anything at all.

But I did hear Mrs. Forth when she started talking again.

"There's a reason why your face is so feminine, you have no visible Adam's apple, your hands are so small, your high waist, your weight distribution, skin, and hair are all more aligned with women than with men . . .

"And that reason is almost certainly because your body was dominated by female hormones as you grew up.

"If you have male genitals that are undersized or malformed, that's the reason for that, too."

Now my face was burning. She was right again—even about the things she couldn't see.

Then I thought the computer screen was getting hazy, but it wasn't the screen, it was my eyes, and I felt the first tear fall when I turned back to Mrs. Forth.

It had taken a long time to sink in, but something finally had.

"Wait!" I exclaimed. "Wait . . . you think I'm . . . a woman? I'm a man!"

Mrs. Forth paused, then visibly relaxed and took on a warmer tone of voice. "Are you a physically normal male, Leo?"

That hurt. It was like she could see through my clothes. She could see what I'd kept secret all my life.

"Yes . . . ! I mean . . . almost. I mean . . . my thing is just a little small, that's all."

My face was still hot, I certainly didn't want to be talking about this, and I felt overwhelmed . . . and even more intimidated.

Maybe that was why I lied, and didn't admit that my thing was extremely small.

"Are your testicles also smaller than normal?" she asked, softly this time.

That felt like a punch to the gut. My testicles were barely a bump, and I was on the verge of crying from both anger and embarrassment.

"Has your fertility been tested?"

The crying feeling vanished, replaced by dizziness. I'd never been to a doctor that I could recall, but . . . this stranger seemed to think she might know that—and more—about me.

"Your face and body are strong evidence that you have female-dominant hormones, and a common reason for that in someone who thinks they're male is that they have intersex genetic anomalies."

Who *think* they're male?

"We support a foundation called Chrysalis, and they can have you tested for intersex genetic mutations and for fertility. At no cost to you. And if that's the case, they can help you adjust to your condition."

My *condition*?

"So," she went on, "the reason you're getting this preliminary interview is because so far, you fit the profile of an intersex person with female dominant hormones and abnormal male genitalia, and who could be an intersex woman . . . if you want to be.

"And if that's the case, and if you want to pursue that, Chrysalis can help you change.

"They can also help you get an account with an exclusive dating service that works well for many intersex people."

"Since you don't seem to be familiar with this, intersex people are physically part man and part woman."

Part man. Not a man. *Part* man.

"If an intersex person appears and acts more masculine than feminine, usually because they have more male parts than female parts, we call them intersex men. If they appear and act feminine, we call them intersex women.

"Which the AI—and I—think you could be, if you want to."

Her phone buzzed and she stopped talking to fiddle with it, and my head was spinning.

Someone else came into the room, but I was too numb to look at them at first.

"Leo, this is Marietta Sinclair, who works for Chrysalis," Mrs. Forth said.

"I'm not qualified to help you deal with this, but Marietta is. The only reason I have this first conversation with applicants like you is because I can talk about things that make some people too uncomfortable.

"And possibly because I never fall apart emotionally out of sympathy—although I didn't mean to imply that about Marietta. She's the best we have."

"Hi, Leo," Marietta said. "I'm so sorry I was late, but I got stuck in a very bad traffic jam.

"If it's okay with you, I'll be your Chrysalis liaison, advisor, coach, and counselor. Every service we provide is completely free, and you can call me, text me, or email anytime of the day or night.

"I'll answer any questions honestly, and if you have any medical questions, we'll cover the costs of any medical tests and of you talking to our doctors, who are some of the best in the world in their fields.

"And if you ask me something I don't know, I'll do my best to find the answer for you."

I was still mentally numb when something changed, and I started feeling serious anger.

"Wait . . . so this was all some kind of bait and switch? You're not offering me training and a job?"

I wanted to jump up and walk out, but for some reason, I couldn't make my body work.

"No, no," Mrs. Forth said. "We'd be happy to offer you free training as a model or as an actress. And like everyone else, we'd be happy to offer you a job if you succeed with your training. Chrysalis is offering to help you in addition to that.

"When this doesn't come as a complete surprise as it has with you, this is when we'd begin the training and job opportunity portion of the interview, but in your case, it might be best if we reschedule that until after you've had time to think all this through."

The two ladies seemed worried about me. Maybe they should be, after microwaving my brain.

Both of them kept talking, but I couldn't take in what they were saying. All my mind could hear, over and over, was "actress." They wanted me to be an *actress*.

Soon after that, Marietta walked with me to the entrance and helped me get in a limo. Somehow I got up to my room and lay down in my bed. I felt like I needed a stiff drink, but I was too stingy to buy alcohol and had other reasons for why I never drank.

Being back in my apartment in the middle of the day felt like a day off—which it was—but in this case, a day off after a long, horrible nightmare.

Was I intersex? That didn't seem possible.

But if it was . . . that could explain a lot.

Could what I had between my legs be explained by being only part male? Could I really be part female, too?

If so . . . could I really be an intersex woman? I wouldn't have thought so, but now I wasn't sure. And if I could be, would I want to be?

Then I realized I was just staring at the ceiling and thinking. Then I didn't care.

Dozens of memories started coming to mind from throughout my life, when I . . . wasn't masculine.

That had always been an annoyance—or worse. A disappointment to myself.

And the countless times I was mistaken for a girl . . .

This intersex idea . . . that could explain all that. Was I intersex all along?

If that was true, and if I wanted to be an intersex woman—if I could—at least I didn't have any family or close friends I'd have to give up to hide that change.

But I would have to get a new job and apartment, and that was very scary. Unless that high-pay claim panned out with Manhattan Talent.

What was I doing?! I was listing pros and cons.

And thinking about the picture of me with makeup, which was now available for me to look at on the app.

And I looked at it a lot.

*

Every time I went to a bathroom I studied my face in the mirror. I bought a small mirror to put in my bedroom. Every time I went on break at work, when I was sure no one else could see, I looked at my AI image again.

Days went by with me upset and wondering things I never wanted to wonder about. The nagging questions interfered with my enjoyment of games and browsing the Internet, and annoyed me while working. But I kept looking at that AI image.

One day while on break at work, I deleted the Manhattan Talent app off my phone so I couldn't look at the image anymore.

Then I pulled out Marietta's business card and texted her. "I don't think I could get used to the idea of living as a woman. Thanks anyway."

A little later, I got a reply.

"That's common, especially if you like your life like it is.

"If you ever change your mind, I'll be here, and remember we have psychologists and therapists who can find out what your exact medical situation is, and help you if you ever change your mind about exploring the option of life as a woman.

"Always with no obligation, and at our expense.

"Best wishes, Marietta"

That gave me relief, and a sense of closure to this misadventure.

And it lasted for several hours.

Until I started thinking about whether or not I liked my life like it is.

*

More days went by with that question cropping up over and over, and I thought about how dissatisfied I was with many things . . .

Dealing with rude, ungrateful customers on the phone . . . my low pay . . . my noisy roommates . . . my tiny room . . .

Working as a model or actress—if I could—would change some of that, and maybe all of it.

But at the cost of living as a woman.

Then one day after a particularly mean customer call, on my way to the breakroom to recover, it hit me—I'd only been thinking about how I like my life as it is right now.

What about in the years to come? What about when I was old and gray? Was this what I wanted for my whole life?!

If I could pass as a woman—a woman who looked good enough to be a model or actress . . . I might be able to earn more money that way. A lot more, maybe.

Would that be easier work? Even fun?

Even if I didn't like pretending to be a woman, could I do it for the money? Would that be any worse than what I was already doing to earn a living?

Or . . . if I was intersex—which now seemed likely to me, despite how much I didn't want it to be true—maybe it wouldn't be pretending. Maybe it would just be switching to the part of me that could make me look like . . . that image.

I downloaded the app again. My phone had kept my login info, and it let me right in. To my makeover image.

Then I began to wonder something else . . . if I was intersex—or maybe even if I wasn't—how could I "explore being a woman?"

Experiment

How does someone—an intersex person—me—go about exploring living as a woman?

I couldn't think of a useful phrase to search for, but I did think of an alternative . . . and I texted Marietta. I wondered if she'd forgotten about me, but I tried anyway.

"Hi Marietta. How would I explore like you talked about?"

Sent. Now wait. A minute went by. Then five. Then ten. Maybe she was busy. Then my phone dinged.

"Hi, Leo. The first step is usually trying on clothes. If you don't like that, then you're unlikely to like any other aspect of changing. I'd be happy to take you shopping, and Chrysalis will buy you an outfit to take home so you can try it as long as you want. Another option is to try makeup. I could help with that, too. -M"

Okay, she remembers me. But clothes . . . makeup . . . ? I wouldn't want to be in a store or a salon looking at those kinds of things. And I'd only want to try them on in my room with the door locked.

I figured out where I could hide a few things in my room for a while . . . but if I was this scared, there's no way I could succeed in changing over.

Well, I'd learned what the first steps were and ruled them out, so I wrote a thanks but never mind message to Marietta.

But I didn't send it. I was kind of curious. So I deleted that reply and started to write another. Then I waffled again.

Twenty minutes later, I sent:

"Thanks, but I don't want to go shopping in public. I might try buying something online someday."

I quickly received a reply.

"May I have your permission to access your account info to get your address and send you an outfit? I think I can guess your size close enough for everything except shoes. If you'll tell me your shoe size, I'll send those, too."

Oh. It'll come to my apartment, and I won't have to pay for it. Hmm.

"Discreet package?" I texted back.

"Completely."

That worked. I sent: "I give permission, and my shoe size is mens 7.5. Thank you!"

Then I sucked in my breath and held it a moment.

I was going to try on women's clothes.

Well . . . I was going to get some. Then I'd see if I had the nerve to actually put them on.

"Since it's Sunday night, delivery probably Tuesday."

I replied: "Thanks. Give me a few days. I'll text you on Thursday."

Her reply was a smiley face.

* * *

I didn't sleep well again, either Sunday or Monday nights.

On Tuesday, I was exhausted at work, and even fell asleep at a table while I was on break. Henry asked me if something was wrong, and I only said I hadn't been sleeping well.

When I got home Tuesday evening, a plain box was waiting for me, but I was sooo tired. I thought about waiting until Thursday—my day off—to even open it.

My nosy apartment mates wanted to know what my package was, and rather than lie and tell them I didn't know, I told them it was a secret.

They enjoyed speculating, but I went into my room and locked the door.

I got the top open, pulled some loose bubble wrap out, and there were several boxes inside. The first one I picked contained a tube of lotion. The second had . . . nylon stockings. Then a pearl necklace.

Next was a dark blue dress with some white bits, and then a black lacy waist belt thing with straps, apparently to hold the stockings up. Then black sandals.

A razor—very fancy and expensive-looking—presumably to shave legs before putting stockings on? And apply the lotion after shaving?

The last three boxes had black lacy panties and matching bra . . . and two rubbery pad things, which I could only guess were meant to pad the bra.

I noted their color was close to the color of my skin.

I put the little boxes and bubble wrap back in the big box to toss down the garbage chute later, and spread the clothes out on my bed.

For a long time, I just stood there, kind of numb. Then I hoped feeling numb wasn't going to become a new habit.

I lay down on top of the clothes—still wearing my regular clothes—and stared at the ceiling.

My brain seemed to be turned off for a while. Maybe due to lack of sleep.

Then I began to think about the clothes, and whether or not I really wanted to try them on.

I didn't want to . . . but I figured I wasn't going to throw them away, and sooner or later, curiosity would drive me to it.

Drag my butt off the bed and get it over with?

No . . . I didn't want to do this that way.

This might be important, and I should give it a fair shot. That meant not tonight, due to mental fatigue.

Either tomorrow after work, or Thursday morning.

When I finally got up, I set about hiding the things where my roommates couldn't find them.

My room didn't have a closet. Instead, it had a clothes rack where I hung my few shirts, pants, jacket, and winter coat, and a box under the bed for underwear and socks.

I put the sandals in my underwear box and covered them up and stuffed everything else into the pockets of my winter coat. Then I realized there was enough room in the many large pockets for the sandals, too, so I moved them.

Sleep came quickly that night, but I woke up early. I decided to take advantage of that and leave before my roommates were likely to get up, and send the big box down the chute.

If one of them did see me with it, I was going to pretend it had some weight in it, like it still had whatever came in it.

I needn't have worried, no one was up when I left.

That day at work wasn't as bad as usual, either. Because I was mildly excited, thinking about what was waiting at home?

On my second work break, Henry came in and started making a cup of tea.

"How are you doing, Leo? You seem happier than usual today."

"Oh, pretty good," I replied. "Slept good last night, I guess."

"Oh, that's very good," Henry said. "Sleep quality's very important to good health."

The thought flashed through my mind to tell him I'd tried the Manhattan Talent app and had passed that first photo audition, but immediately ruled that out.

First, there were other coworkers in there. Second . . . that would lead to lots of questions about what happened next, and that was to be avoided at all costs.

Finally, my shift was over, and I felt unusually lighthearted while walking to my subway station.

I figured when I got home would be a good time to try on the clothes and make a decision one way or the other about whether or not I'd try any further "exploring."

Then my thoughts shifted way ahead . . . if I ever decided to really live as a woman . . .

Just then my train arrived. I got on, took a seat, and opened my phone to send Marietta a text:

"I'd have to change my name?"

Then right after I hit the send button, I fussed at myself. It implied I was seriously considering changing my whole life, and I wasn't seriously considering changing anything yet.

I was thinking and acting impulsively, and that wasn't like me.

My phone dinged.

"Sooner or later, if you decide to become an intersex woman . . . Leo is definitely not a feminine name."

All of a sudden I was feeling angsty, and I wanted to quit thinking about all this.

I wished I hadn't texted Marietta at all, so . . . I texted back to try to end this topic:

"I'm not a creative person. I don't think I could come up with a suitable name."

"Michelle," came a quick reply. "The first moment I saw you, I wanted to call you that. No obligation, of course. And I can come up with other choices for you."

So much for ending the topic.

I stared at my phone. Michelle . . . I opened the app and stared at my makeover picture. With a "highly feminine" face. Michelle . . . It sounded perfect . . . for someone who looked like that. If I decided to look like that. If, if, if . . .

"Last name?" I texted. Asking wasn't a conscious decision, it was automatic, somehow, and it didn't even occur to me that I could keep my last name.

The next reply was a few minutes later. "What kind of feeling would you like it to have? Traditional? Common? Unusual? Feminine? Sexy? Fictional?"

"Feminine," I wrote after a minute or two.

I had a much longer wait this time.

Then the reply came: "Michelle Loren."

The instant I read it, I started breathing faster. Harder. It was like I recognized something . . . like I had discovered a hidden treasure.

Michelle Loren.

A follow-up text came moments later: "Stress the last syllable. lor-EN. Like Sophia Loren."

I didn't text anymore that night, and instead of getting my hidden clothes out right away, I spent a lot of time looking at my makeover image and the mirror, while thinking about the name Michelle Loren.

After a while, I lay down on my bed.

Nothing made sense.

I was attracted to a feminine image of me . . . and to a feminine name . . . but I didn't feel feminine at all. And I not only wasn't attracted to men, I was repelled by the idea of dating one.

This was the perfect time to try on those clothes, but I wasn't eager to do it.

Why not? Was I scared I'd like them? Scared I wouldn't? Or . . . was I trying to build more anticipation, maybe?

Hours went by with me idling between the image, the mirror, and thinking about that name. And over that time, something began to change.

I began to warm to the idea that the image was me.

That all I had to do was grow my hair out and learn to put on a little makeup, and it wouldn't be an AI fake anymore, it'd really be me. And . . . if I wanted . . .

I could be Michelle Loren.

When I started getting undressed for bed, I briefly considered putting on the new clothes, but just as quickly decided I'd do it tomorrow after I had my morning toast and coffee.

So . . . I lay down to go to sleep, but my mind resisted a while . . . Michelle Loren. The image. Me.

I was aware of half-waking several times, always with the same thoughts.

And they were still there when I woke up the next morning, and while I ate.

After breakfast, once I was safely ensconced in my room, I started to get out the new clothes, but paused.

On a whim, I moved my bed until it was against the door in case someone tried to open it and the lock didn't work. Then I got all my new clothes out and put them on the bed.

I took off my shoes, socks, and pants, but left my underwear and shirt on.

There was an instruction sheet in the razor box, and it said to use running water, but I decided to try dry shaving so I wouldn't get questioned about spending too much time in the bathroom.

First I examined my legs carefully and decided to only shave the coarse hair, which was only on the front half of my shins.

I started with my left leg, and since I was dry shaving, I went with the grain, not against it. I was surprised that it worked well, and didn't hurt.

Then I did the other shin. I had no idea how long it would take to grow back, but I was confident no one would ever see my shins. I didn't even own a pair of short pants.

I slipped my underpants off and tried to figure out the best order to put the clothes on, but gave up and picked up the panties. I was standing, then bent over, just about to put one foot in, but paused. It seemed like a momentous occasion.

I took a deep breath, stepped into them, pulled them all the way up, and was stunned.

As they slid up and settled into place, I gasped.

I felt more aroused than I ever had before.

I was breathing hard, almost panting. My little thing was making a bump, and the silk or nylon or whatever it was felt . . . sensuous.

I just stood still a long time with those sensations etching themselves into my brain.

Eventually, I picked up a stocking and sat on the edge of the bed. I was a bit clumsy, but I got it on. It didn't give me the same feeling as the panties had, maybe because it was harder.

I did a little better with the other stocking, and was pretty sure I'd be even better next time.

I got the belt thing and slid it up and onto my waist. It had a size adjustment, and I made it snug, which I figured it had to be to do its job.

I finally figured out how to fasten the belt's straps to the stockings, and I did it. When I stood up, I had to adjust them, but I'd remember how to do it better next time.

Then I took a step, and stopped in shock.

Another step, another shock.

I only had space to walk the length of my bed plus one step, but I went back and forth and started crying—very quietly. Why I cried, I have no idea, but I did.

I kept crying as I took off my shirt and struggled to figure out how to put the bra on, using the smallest set of hooks, and then I fiddled around with the inserts until I seemed to have them right.

The little mirror in my room was too small to see much at one time, but it helped a little.

Then I stood still with my eyes closed, still crying . . . just thinking about the fact that I was wearing nothing but women's clothing.

Then I lay face down on my bed and used my pillow to muffle my sobs. I cried long and hard, although I didn't know why I was crying at all.

Then I thought I hadn't cried since my mother died . . . and that I was crying almost as hard as I had then.

When I'd calmed down to quiet crying again, I felt really tired. I also remembered I needed to update Marietta today.

My phone was within reach, so I got it and tried to think of what to write. I couldn't think well enough to be cautious in how I phrased things, so I just wrote what first came to mind.

"I just tried on the clothes. Just underclothes. Still wearing them. Now what?"

While I was waiting what seemed like a long time—but might not have been—I felt like an idiot. Obviously, the next thing was to put on the dress and shoes.

"Do you like them?" Marietta texted.

"I don't know. I'm crying, and I don't know why. I almost never cry."

"Did putting them on feel good? Do they feel good now?"

I typed, "Very good when I put on panties" and paused, worried about putting that in writing, but gave up and went on. "Very good when I put on panties. Struggled with rest. Very good when I moved in them. Not much feeling good or bad when lying still."

"Are you wearing the dress on top of them?"

"No."

"Try that. Walk like that. See how that feels."

I sat up, got the dress, found a zipper in the back and unzipped it. I didn't know if I should step into it and pull it up or pull it on over my head.

I went with stepping into it, but it felt very, very strange.

Putting on my normal clothes was always automatic, never requiring any thought. This was new, and I was hyper sensitive to every sensation as I put my arms in and started trying to contort myself enough to get it zipped up in back.

Once I had it, I straightened up and took a few breaths to calm down. I was too anxious to put on the shoes.

I took my first few steps in the dress and was stunned again. I wondered if this was like what people felt when they had sex. I struggled to keep going because the sensations were so strong and getting stronger, but I couldn't have stopped if I'd wanted to.

In no more than a minute or two, I was overwhelmed with intense feelings and started shaking violently, collapsing to the floor, and I ended up in almost a fetal position.

This was crazy. I didn't even have the strength to get up for a while.

This couldn't be normal. Women walk around like normal, they don't collapse every few steps. There must be something seriously wrong with me.

I felt a wet spot and thought I must've peed a little.

I thought about texting Marietta and asking for help, but I was on the floor and my phone was on the bed.

Slowly, I calmed down, started to relax, and felt my strength returning. I wasn't dying. Maybe I was just overstimulated?

When I felt like getting up again, I could pace back and forth again and see if I handled it better, worse, or just the same.

If it was the same or worse, this was obviously not something I could pull off, even for a high paying job.

Easing up into a sitting position went without calamity, and so did standing up. Walking a few paces felt really good, but not too good.

Cautious about not overdoing it again, I sat down on the bed and then lay down to relax and recover some more.

I never expected anything like this.

I reached for my phone but just held it as I thought about what to say. I didn't want to go into detail, so I settled on "It feels better than I ever felt before," but it was a few more minutes before I typed it in and sent it.

She replied quickly. "I'm glad you found something you like. Just a reminder, if you want to get tested or talk to our psychologist, just let me know."

"Both, please. As soon as possible," I replied without thinking.

Again, I'd acted impulsively, and chastised myself for it, but as I thought it over, I figured I would've decided the same thing no matter how long I took to consider it.

"What are some good days and times?" she replied.

"Any time on any Thursday. Is that okay?"

"That's great. I'll get with their staff to set you up. Do you want to meet and talk now? Or we can keep chatting if you prefer."

This time I took a minute before replying, "I think I want to stay home and quiet for the rest of today, if you don't mind."

"Of course I don't. But don't hesitate to text me if you need anything."

A little while later I put on the sandals, which had higher heels than I was used to, and paced a little in them. It was strange, but okay, and I didn't have a repeat of being overstimulated.

When I started to take off my new clothes, I got the dress off and realized if I sat down on a toilet with my clothes like this, the straps connected to the stockings would prevent my panties from going all the way down.

But rearranging was for next time.

I finished undressing, re-hid the clothes, and moved the bed back to its normal place and went back to normal.

Well, maybe not. Maybe I was changing whether I wanted to or not.

It was a regular day off, but not an ordinary one, not after starting like this. So I decided to do something else I'd never done before—I took the subway to Central Park and spent a few hours there.

And that night I slept better than I had in a long, long, time.

Genes

On my first break at work the next morning, I had gotten a text from Marietta giving me the time of my appointment with their psychologist.

She also asked if I needed a limo to get there or back home, and asked me to go into the app—into a medical section that was just for Chrysalis clients.

The doc's office was very close to a subway station, so I passed on a limo.

The medical part asked me to approve Chrysalis doctors sharing medical records between them and asked me to go to a walk-in lab to have blood drawn.

The lab company had an office only a couple of subway stops from where I worked, and they had late hours, so I went there on the way home. I didn't have to pay, and they collected blood, urine, and spit.

After that, I texted Marietta on the way home and told her I'd been to the lab. She replied and asked how I was feeling.

I thought about that before replying.

"My brain feels like it's turned off, and I'm just going through motions. I put some of my new underthings on under my pants this morning, but I was too afraid of getting caught, so I took them off. Then I almost cried on the way to work because I wanted them. Am I going crazy?"

"No," she replied. "You're just starting to learn how to adjust to something you never expected. Would you like me to go with you to your doctor's appointment?"

"Yes, please. If you don't mind."

I didn't have to think twice about that.

Then she asked about my family and close friends. I told her my mom was dead, I never knew my father, and I never had any close friends.

Hours later, Marietta texted and asked if I could arrive at nine for an ultrasound test, and I agreed. It was at the same clinic with the doctors.

Every night before the doctor's appointment, I locked my bedroom door, moved the bed against it, and put my new clothes on again.

And for the first time in my life, I paid attention to my breasts.

I knew they were curvier than most guys, but I'd always assumed they were just a little flabby because I never exercise.

But now . . . I wondered about the difference between men and women regarding the size of nipples and the dark circles around them . . . and where mine fit in a comparison like that.

* * *

On Thursday, the ultrasound was extremely embarrassing.

I was naked except for a thin robe that opened in the front, and an older woman pushed and prodded the ultrasound probe all around my crotch and all the way up to where my ribs started, while someone else watched the screens over her shoulder.

After that, I went back to the waiting room, where Marietta was. Sometime later a nurse called us back to a doctor's office.

"Hi, Leo, I'm Dr. Crowley, your psychologist, and this is Dr. Benton, your clinical geneticist."

Crowley was a man, and Benton was a lady doctor.

We sat down and Dr. Crowley said, "Leo, in my profession, we generally prefer to ask questions to help you discover things about yourself, including problem areas, and what you might do to improve them.

"However, since this may be our only meeting, I'm going to give you a lot of information now. You won't be able to remember it all, but you're welcome to call me or message me if and when you have questions later, and I'll get back to you as soon as I can.

"Does that sound reasonable to you?"

I noticed I was breathing hard, which made me self-conscious, but I managed an automatic, "Yes."

"Dr. Benton's here because the tests we had done showed some anomalies. The ultrasound confirmed them."

I raised my eyebrows, but I couldn't think of a response before Dr. Benton spoke up.

"You have ovotesticular syndrome, Leo . . . a rare genetic condition that means you're biologically intersex . . . part male and part female."

It was true? It was really true . . . ?

"Wait . . ." I managed to say, "you mean I actually have female body parts? Where?"

Marietta rested a hand on my forearm.

"In addition to your testes, you also have ovaries," Dr. Benton said gently. "You have testes, as you know, but they're only about fifteen percent of normal size and not descended, and your ovaries are almost normal size.

"So all your life you've had less testosterone and more estrogens than a normal male."

"Wow . . ." I muttered. I took a deep breath and let it out.

Dr. Benton went on, "With that, and your hormone profile and testicular function tested through your blood panels, we can predict with a high degree of confidence that you're sterile . . ."

That literally took my breath away for a moment. I felt like I might faint, but that morphed into fighting tears.

I don't know why I took it so hard, because I'd never dated and never expected to . . . because I knew I physically didn't have what it would take to satisfy a girl.

But regardless of all that, this news felt like I'd just lost something very important.

Something very personal.

When I'd recovered some, Dr. Crowley said, "We know of more than thirty genetic variations—plus other triggers—that can make someone intersex.

"Some use a narrow definition: only cases where chromosomes, testes or ovaries, or external genitals don't fit simple male or female. That includes you."

Me.

"OT syndrome shows up in roughly one in twenty thousand births, so in New York City, with eight and a half million people, that's about four hundred people walking around with the same condition.

"Add every narrow condition together and you hit fifteen hundred New Yorkers. Many of them know it—because doctors often catch their ambiguities at birth.

"Then there's the broader view that includes all sex traits that vary from the textbook male or female.

"Symptoms can be obvious at birth, hide inside, surface late, or barely register. Ninety percent of them never hear the word intersex applied to themselves. Of the ten percent who do, most keep living the gender that matches their dominant organs; it's simply easier.

Dominant organs . . . ? What are mine?

"The intersex people who switch genders are usually the ones raised against their dominant organs, or they're close to half-and-half. Those are the rarest of the rare."

"But if you count every variation under the broad view, you reach one and a half percent of the population—roughly a hundred fifty thousand New Yorkers. Not rare at all.

Everyone was quiet a long time.

"What . . . what does all that mean to me . . ." I finally asked.

"You've lived your life so far as a male," Dr. Crowley said. "You can keep doing that, now with an awareness that your hormones affect you differently than other men.

"Or, if you feel more feminine than masculine, you could start living as a female—in which case Chrysalis will help you adjust."

Marietta added, "And you can have a free membership at the Aurum Dating Service. They welcome intersex members, and they work closely with Chrysalis."

They were all quiet again, so they were apparently waiting on me to say something, so I said the first thing that came to mind.

"Do I have to do the dating service to, uh, use the other Chrysalis . . . services?

"Oh, no," Marietta said, "we'll help you no matter what. Manhattan Talent and Chrysalis were both started by an intersex woman. She also started Aurum."

That almost fried my brain. A lot of puzzle pieces just jumped together all at once.

"We have a training and adjustment campus in the Hamptons," Marietta continued.

"You're welcome to come there for a tour, and if you ever want to start living as a woman, you can live there for free while you get used to it."

"And we have a lot of experience helping patients make those adjustments," Dr. Crowley said.

"As you start adapting to all this new information about yourself, it's important to realize you don't have to conform to stereotypes about what's masculine or feminine.

"Most people have a mix of masculine and feminine behaviors, attitudes, and traits, with one set being dominant and aligning with their biological sex, with a few opposite-sex traits, but a few come close to half-and-half.

"Since your biology is mixed, it may not be easy or fast for you to determine your long-term preferences."

I'm . . . mixed . . .

"The choices of what suits you best are yours and yours alone, but since those choices can feel overwhelming, I can help you explore your feelings with a goal toward helping you decide how to spend the rest of your life."

"Dang . . ."

Whatever else was said, I don't remember, but after that meeting, Marietta took me to a restaurant for lunch.

* * *

After ordering, Marietta said, "I agree with what Dr. Crowley said about not having to conform to stereotypes, but after your first reactions to wearing women's clothes, I have an idea . . .

"If you'd like, there's a ladies fashion store that works with Manhattan Talent, and we could go shopping there after we finish eating.

"It's where your first outfit came from, and Chrysalis will pay for you to get some more outfits for you to try, if you'd like that."

"I . . . I need to think about that," I said.

"Okay. And while we're waiting for the food, do you mind if I check my messages while you think?"

I agreed, and started reflecting on how fast I went from always knowing I was male to beginning to consider . . . something else.

Although I'd learned as a child I wasn't a normal male, I just thought I was an unusual male.

The idea of being intersex was unnerving, at first. But when everything about that possibility seemed to match reality . . . I guess I was beginning to accept that.

And now that I'd found out I have ovaries . . . well, there was no more doubting my biology.

Now . . . what was I going do with this new information?

The AI had been right about the possibility of me being intersex, and how pretty I could look.

If all I had to do to look feminine—very feminine—was long hair and a little makeup . . .

If I could earn a lot more money by doing that . . .

And my first few times wearing women's clothes went sort of okay—except for that first wild reaction . . .

Did I enjoy wearing those clothes? Yes, but . . . that could just be the novelty of it.

At that moment I realized two contradictory things: I wanted to wear them again. And I still didn't want my roommates or coworkers to know.

Now I knew I wanted to take the offer of more clothes, but I couldn't—because circumstances overruled what I wanted.

When our food was served, Marietta put her phone down, and I said, "Thanks for the offer of more clothes, but that won't work.

"I have nosy roommates and barely found places to hide what you already gave me."

"You're not the first intersex client we've had with that issue, and this boutique has nondescript locking boxes in various sizes. We'll buy you one of those at the same time, if you'd like."

We ate in silence while I thought about it.

It was hard for me to believe I had actually put on panties and stockings, and the rest . . . or that I had liked it.

But I had, in fact, liked it.

I felt guilty for liking it, but I liked it despite that.

And the idea of getting more was . . . exciting, although realizing that was scary.

"I . . . that's very generous, but I don't think that would help . . . my biggest problem's that I don't have anywhere to wear them.

"I'm afraid to wear them out of my room, and my room's barely big enough for my twin-size bed."

"Our campus is perfect for that," Marietta said. "You could live there for free, or you could store your clothes in a locker there and just wear them when you come to visit.

"The campus is large and beautiful, like a garden park, and that's where I work most of the time."

"Oh? You travel all the way to the Hamptons?"

"No, I live there. I just come into the city sometimes, for clients like you."

She glanced around and lowered her quiet voice even more.

"I was once a Chrysalis intersex client, too. Long before they used computers to help find us.

"My genetic condition isn't exactly the same as yours . . . but Chrysalis and the Aurum Dating Service helped me find a wonderful, loving husband who loves me as I am.

"We live in the Hamptons because I wanted to work at our campus, and my husband's independently wealthy and liked the area.

"Although it's a relatively small house because . . . I can't have children. I have a vagina, but no uterus.

"We've considered adopting or fostering, but . . . that would be too emotionally painful for me."

I felt like crying out of sympathy, but held it off, and we ate in silence again.

Marietta was the one who finally said something again.

"So . . . may I take you shopping, and then take you to visit the campus, show you around, explain things, and get you a locker for your new clothes?"

I nodded.

I wasn't sure why, and that bothered me, but something in me wouldn't let me turn down her invitation again.

For a moment I wondered if it was because all I had to do otherwise was go home and play Pokémon, but I quickly realized it felt like it was much more than that—whatever it was.

The boutique had several private areas, and Marietta and I were in one of them, so I wasn't in a crowded store with a bunch of strangers around—which went a long way toward reducing my anxiety.

We spent over two hours there, but it wasn't a shopping spree, and I didn't leave with armloads of shopping bags.

It was Marietta and one saleswoman named Carol showing me things and explaining them, and me trying on different kinds of things and gazing at myself in full-length mirrors.

One corner had a set of three full-length mirrors where the middle one stayed put and the other two could sort of wrap around some, so I could see how I looked from the sides and partly from the back.

Much of the time I felt strange, like I was in someone else's body, and I had a lot of little crises, like mini panic attacks, where my feelings alternated between happiness and fear, and I teared up some, for both reasons . . .

But all those strange feelings mostly ended when I looked in the corner mirrors after Carol fitted me with a hairpiece in my hair color, but with long, wavy hair. Something major changed.

The fear dimmed, and a new feeling started taking its place—a feeling of peace.

I looked like the girl the AI had made from my actual photo—minus the makeup . . . and I wasn't confused anymore.

Dazed, but not confused.

I accepted the fact that what I was looking at was me . . . and I wasn't afraid of that anymore.

I was even able to consider my looks with a little objectivity.

My face looked okay because right before leaving home, I'd shaved my little bit of facial hair—mostly light, slightly long sideburns that grew slowly enough that it wouldn't start to show for at least a couple of days.

What I was doing started feeling less exotic, and more . . . natural. It seemed like maybe this was right for me.

After Carol and Marietta got through with me in the store, I hugged them both a long time, and I did tear up again then, but it was out of gratitude.

I left with the hairpiece, three pairs of panties, three bras, two different size bra inserts, two pairs of stockings, one waist garter belt, one beautiful black dress, a pair of black dress shoes with one-inch heels, and just in case—a box of tissues.

It all would've fit in a single bag, but they put it in two, and the bags were unlabeled and generic-looking.

Campus

Marietta paid attention to traffic as her Tesla did most of the driving up Long Island to the Hamptons, but it made it easy for her to talk, and she told me a lot.

"Chrysalis is on the privately owned campus of the Manhattan Talent Retreat and it's a wonderful place.

"It has medical facilities, dining, several lounges, a salon, a heated indoor pool, a gym, fashion and acting training rooms, and two dozen apartments.

"Outside there are covered patios, lots of pretty lawn areas, trees, walking paths with benches, fountains, and flower gardens."

"Oh, that all sounds wonderful," I said.

"And being in the Hamptons and away from the main road, it's quiet outside," Marietta replied. "Oh, and shuttles to the beach in the summers. It's like a high-class resort in many ways."

"What . . . what do . . . clients . . . do there?"

"Well, for Chrysalis clients like you, anything and everything that helps them adjust to a new way of life.

"But you don't just live there and hope you adjust—we have extensive courses available, some online and some in person, and it's completely customized for each person."

"I think I'd need a lot of guidance. How likely would I be to see you sometimes?"

"If you live on campus? Every day for a while, and as your coach, I'd be responsible for customizing your feminine training.

"If you want to interview for fashion and acting, and if you pass that—which you probably would—you'd have other people in charge of that kind of training.

"Most of Manhattan Talent's fashion and acting candidates already have a lot of training, but the ones who come to the campus either need some extra training, or they have the looks but no training.

"We provide whatever might help them become successful at those careers so we can earn commissions when we get them jobs.

"We also have boarding students here who pay to take classes. They haven't had or haven't passed one of our auditions, but they're willing to pay for the training anyway."

"So you have clients . . . students . . . and candidates?" I asked.

"Yes . . . one person can have more than one label, but the way we use the terms, candidates are people who've passed our audition interview and live here while taking classes.

"The people who pay for classes, we call students . . . and the people Chrysalis hosts here we call clients.

"But to avoid segregation, the staff calls all of them residents, so other residents won't know why you're there unless you tell them.

"And the people there to learn fashion and acting usually aren't aware that there are intersex people on campus.

"Oh, and some clients are also called members, if they join the Aurum Dating Service—which is free for Chrysalis clients."

"Aurum? What does that mean?" I asked.

"Oh, that's Latin for gold. It has a lot of very wealthy members—called prime members—who pay big fees to be in it. People who can't afford the prime fees can apply for a low-fee membership, but the acceptance rate is very, very low. They're called standard members or usually just members."

"Oh. So, odds are I wouldn't get in?"

"No, no. Chrysalis does the Aurum screening for our clients, and we've never had one not qualify as a standard member."

"Really . . . ? Wow."

"By the way," Marietta added, "every ADS member has a dating coach, and is required to complete ADS courses.

"And for every Chrysalis client who joins the dating service, your Chrysalis coach is also your dating coach."

"Oh, nice. Um . . .

"If I decided to, uh, change completely, how long would that take?"

Her next reply took longer, but it came.

"That depends on what you consider 'completely.' Many clients at Chrysalis have gone through internal struggles long before they found us, and this is relatively easy for them . . .

"For you, it will take longer. Maybe six months to a year, or even longer. But you can live at the Chrysalis campus while you do it, all expenses paid."

All expenses? For a year?! At a resort?

Did I follow Alice into Wonderland?

I felt myself relaxing, and only then realized I'd been tense—maybe all day.

Talking to Marietta—or just listening to her—was soothing.

"Fashion and acting residents are usually on campus from a couple of weeks to a few months," she was saying, "depending on how promising they are and how much help they need. Chrysalis residents stay much longer—as long as they need.

"For you, you'll have counseling several times a week—more if needed—surgical changes if wanted, electrolysis, training . . .

"Typically, about ninety percent of our few Chrysalis residents are adapting to try to live as women.

"We have three of those right now, and we had one learning how to live as a man last year."

"Oh, really? So I wouldn't be the only one."

"No, there are almost always several on campus. You don't have to socialize with them, but after you've started getting comfortable with things, you might like to.

"You're all part of a very exclusive club, biologically, and everyone usually gets along very well with each other."

"Hmm . . . I wouldn't have to decide right away about something like that, right?"

"Right."

"And all the custom courses . . . what kind of things would that entail? It can't be much, can it?"

Marietta chuckled.

"Training for you would include functional things like makeup, skin care, hair care, nail care, voice, walking in heels . . .

"And it includes behavioral training like feminine mannerisms, etiquette, and attitudes . . .

"And practicalities, like how to choose and use different kinds of handbags and purses, and feminine sexuality . . ."

Okay, so it could be much. Very much. That was a little intimidating.

We were both quiet a while as the car kept humming along, until I commented on one of the last things she'd said.

"I don't feel very sexual. That might not be possible for me."

She didn't reply right away, so we were quiet again, but this time Marietta broke the silence.

"You said the first time you wore women's underclothes and a dress felt better than anything you ever felt before. Did that feel sexual?"

I felt my face get hot. I reluctantly admitted, "Yeah, it did. And it was . . . very . . . nice."

After a long pause, Marietta said, "Hormones play an important role in feeling sexual. You've had less than normal male hormones, but probably close to normal female hormones.

"Maybe you've never felt sexual because you've always lived as a man, and by doing that you automatically suppressed feminine thoughts and desires.

"Maybe you'll start to feel more of a normal level of sexuality if you live at Chrysalis a while . . .

"When we get there, would you like to change into some of your new clothes and wear them while I give you a tour?"

"I'd be too nervous," I said after a long pause. "I think I'd like to look around first."

* * *

We chatted more until she turned onto the campus and waited for the gate to swing open, and the place was huge. Not huge buildings, but lots and lots of trees and grass.

She explained and pointed out the different buildings and said that all the doctors and staff lived on Long Island.

We put my new clothes in a locker, and then she took me to an empty residential suite—and it was incredible!

It was bigger than the whole apartment where I lived, but it only had one bedroom—a *big* bedroom—with a *queen*-size bed—and everything looked expensive.

The whole tour only took about half an hour, ending at the lockers and changing rooms between the swimming pool and the gym.

"Would you like me to drive you home now?" Marietta asked.

I hesitated.

She'd already driven all the way into the city and back just for me. I could let her drop me at a train station to save her from having to make the whole trip twice in one day.

But . . . what I had to go home to seemed less appealing than ever.

"Would you like to put your new clothes on . . . ? Marietta asked. "The changing rooms are large enough for me to come in and help you with the hairpiece and anything else you need."

I kept hesitating.

"After you change into your new clothes, I'll walk you to the dining facility, we'll have a dessert, and I'll walk you back here. And you won't have to talk to anyone but me. How does that sound?"

It sounded terrifying . . . but I nodded.

Marietta stayed in the changing room with me the whole time, and I cried a bit and appreciated the tissues the store had given me.

When there was nothing left to put on or adjust, Marietta put my old clothes in a locker, came right back, and held the changing room door open for me.

I came out and stood just outside the changing room, breathing hard and half-expecting a panic attack.

It wasn't the clothes—it was that someone besides Marietta might see me.

We stepped outside the door of the changing area into a hallway, and I leaned back against the wall next to the door to catch my breath.

There were other people around. Some passing by, some heading our way, and some walking away. Most paid us no attention. One lady in a staff uniform glanced at me and smiled and nodded as she passed by.

Marietta was steadily talking to me in a very quiet, gentle voice, but I was too scared to pay attention to the words.

When no one else was nearby for a minute, Marietta took my arm in hers, and we started walking. Slowly.

Walking felt funny.
And awkward.
And conspicuous.

It didn't feel anything like it had felt when I was pacing in my bedroom at home . . . until it did.

All of a sudden, I became keenly sensitive to my panties and stockings, and the weight and subtle motion of the bra inserts, and I gasped as I stopped walking.

"Is this too much?" Marietta asked, turning as if to walk me back the short distance to the changing rooms.

"Keep . . . going . . ." I whispered. "Slowly."
I took a step, leaning on Marietta.
Another step.
Another.
I took several, and stopped again.
I repeated that, taking a few more steps each time.

There, in a hallway, wearing long hair, a dress, and everything under it, when no one else was around, I stopped and whispered, "I feel sexual, Marietta. I feel very sexual."

When we got to the dining area, Marietta took us to an out-of-the-way booth. A waitress appeared and Marietta asked for two dessert menus.

The dining facility was impressive.

There was an elegant open area with nothing between the tables, but the rest of the seating was in a maze of booths separated by high walls.

There was a limited self-serve area, or a larger selection through the waitstaff.

Marietta asked me if I'd chosen something, and I replied that there was too much to choose from.

"Chocolate ice cream, then?" she asked, and I nodded.

The waitress reappeared, and Marietta ordered for both of us.

"May I call you Michelle while you're dressed this way?" Marietta asked.

I thought it over and nodded again, too embarrassed to say it out loud.

"Michelle, have you ever noticed that you have a strong preference for others to make decisions for you, or to help you make decisions?"

This time I nodded without hesitation, and I answered, too.

"Yes . . . that's annoyed me my whole life. I don't know why I'm like that. And I've tried to change that, but . . . I obviously failed."

Marietta smiled. "Are you aware that's a feminine trait? Very feminine."

My mind whirled. "Really . . . ?" I finally replied.

"Yes. It's a decision-making style called dependent or interpersonally-oriented. It's very common among women, and very rare among men."

"Dang . . ."

"You've been relying on me a lot to make decisions, which isn't a bad thing, but it's important for you to be aware of that. Especially since you have some very important decisions to make that will affect the rest of your life."

The rest of my life.

There was that phrase again. I sighed deeply.

*

We finished dessert and walked back to the changing area.

I didn't need any help walking this time, despite an unfamiliar but rapidly increasing feeling of sexuality.

When we got there, Marietta got my old clothes out of my locker and held open a changing room door for me . . . but I froze outside the door.

Tears started down my face, without me making any noise.

"Do you want to stay dressed this way?" Marietta asked softly.

I nodded.

She furrowed her brow in thought.

"Do you want to stay here tonight?"

I shook my head vigorously, the tears coming faster.

"I can't. I have to work tomorrow, and I can't risk being late. If I get fired, I'll be homeless . . ."

"Do you want to start living here? Right now?"

I shook my head again.

"I can't. This is just temporary, and if I lose my job and my rented room . . . I'll have nothing to go back to."

Marietta walked me to the closest lounge and we sat on a short sofa in a corner.

"You want to stay, but you can't," she said, "because your housing and finances wouldn't be secure . . ."

I nodded.

"What if I can make your long-term housing and finances secure?"

I'd been gazing at the floor, but I quickly turned to look at her. "I don't understand . . ."

"I can authorize you to move in right now," she said, "so that's not a problem.

"Based on our history, you have an excellent chance of leaving here happily married, like I did, but we need to make sure you're taken care of even if that doesn't happen. Here's how we can do that . . .

"If you want or need to leave here on your own, you can live with Charles and I as long as you want.

"We have a very nice guest room, and we'll provide your meals, too.

"That means you won't need any money except for incidentals or to save money for your future, but for that, you can earn an income by working here. I have the authority to guarantee that, too."

I fell against Marietta and bawled.

She wrapped her arms around me until I couldn't cry any more, and I just panted a few minutes.

"I miss my momma," I whimpered, the thought coming out of the blue.

When I finally sat up, I was lightheaded.

"I'll show you the other empty suites and let you choose your favorite, and you can stay there while I take care of some things.

"Then I'll go over some business things with you, including helping you get through ending your job and your lease . . .

"Tomorrow morning one of our drivers will go with you in a van with some empty boxes and he'll help you pack all your belongings and bring them back here.

"You can dress like Leo for that trip so you can say goodbye to your roommates.

"Then when you get back here, we'll start your feminine training by shopping for a whole wardrobe, all paid for by Chrysalis.

"Carol and I will help you choose a good set of clothes from the same shop where she works—all by video call—and she'll make sure you get the right sizes. Then it will all be delivered to your suite here.

"I'm your assigned counselor, and I'll be with you for hours every morning and afternoon as long as you need me that much, and you'll slowly start trying new things, like learning what kinds of makeup there are, what they're for, how to apply them, and how to take them off.

"Does all that sound okay?"
I nodded in a daze.

"Do you have any questions?"
I shook my head.

"Ready to choose your suite?"
I nodded.

As Marietta showed me the available suites, I began to get more of my wits about me again, and was embarrassed.

I said something about that, and she told me I was dealing with a lot of profound changes, and that I was doing fine.

I chose a suite on the second floor with a great view, giving up my second choice of a first-floor suite with a walkout door to a garden.

Before Marietta left me for a while, she told me that starting the day after next, she wanted me to have dinner with her and Charles every other evening, to help me start learning to socialize as Michelle.

After she left, I ambled around the suite in a mental fog.
I just gave up my job.
I just gave up my room in the city.
I just gave up dressing as a man.
I just gave up my man's name.

But I had a beautiful new suite, and when I had to leave, I'd move to Marietta's guest room and start working here. Or maybe even a fashion or acting job.

And the craziest thing of all was that I even had a dim possibility that I could adapt to feeling like a woman enough that I'd be able to marry a man and be happy as his wife.

*

That night, I took a bath and soaked in the hot water—which the tub circulated and kept at a constant temperature.

No roommates who needed me to get out of the bathroom.

Then I noticed something.

I was naked, the same as I'd been when I took countless hurried showers over the years.

I never felt male or female all those times, but now . . . sitting there, soaking in that hot water, in a luxury suite, all by myself . . . I felt . . . female. I felt feminine.

It was a strange, foreign feeling . . . but a very nice one.

Changes

The next morning I dressed as Leo and the chatty van driver drove us into the city, leaving at 5 a.m. to avoid rush hour traffic.

He told me, among a hundred other unrelated things, that he always fell in love with every "new woman" at Chrysalis, but he could only date one if they asked him for a date.

Did he know I was a Chrysalis client, and might become one of those new women?

Was he hoping I'd ask him?

That question made me wonder what it would be like for a man to ask me for a date while I looked like Michelle.

And then . . . I wondered what it would be like to actually date a guy—and I couldn't imagine it at all.

But then . . . I had rarely imagined dating a woman, either.

We got to my old apartment early enough that two of my roommates were still there for me to say goodbye to, and packing only took about five minutes.

The driver could unfold a new box and have it ready in a few seconds, and all my clothes only took two medium-size boxes, with room to spare.

The only other items were my used handheld game machine, a few toiletry items, and a few trinkets on a shelf.

Next he drove me to my old workplace and waited while I went in to sign some papers and say goodbye to friends.

When they asked what I was going to do instead, I told them it was confidential and I'd promised not to talk about it.

That was true, because Marietta had made me promise her . . . after I told her I wanted an excuse not to tell my roommates and coworkers.

Henry seemed very emotional when we said goodbye.

He handed me a folded sheet of paper, shook my hand, said he'd like me to stay in touch, and said he hoped I'd be very happy. It seemed way over the top compared to everyone else.

*

While the driver chatted idly on the way back to Chrysalis, I took out the paper Henry gave me, unfolded it, and read a quickly scribbled note.

Leo,

We've always had high turnover here, but you and I have been here longer than most, and I didn't realize until now how much I look forward to seeing you here.

I'll really miss you, and I hope things work out very well for you.

I'll always be your friend.

—Henry

It ended with his signature and personal contact information, and my eyes watered. Then they watered in streams down my face, while the driver chatted on regardless.

It was the only letter I'd ever gotten from anyone.

Maybe it was my fault for always being a loner, but Henry was now the only person who ever told me he looked forward to seeing me. Or that he'd miss me. Or that he hoped things would work out well for me. Or . . . that he was my friend.

I was aware that women in general were more prone to crying, presumably due to female hormones, but even though I had lots of those, I'd had them all along, so why was I becoming so emotional so frequently lately?

Regardless of my hormones or genes, I didn't want to be the kind of person who cried a lot. So, I tried changing what I was thinking about.

The car noises hummed us along while I began some serious thinking about my long-term future, and that wasn't something I was used to. But at least it didn't make me cry.

*

When we got back to campus, I immediately changed into my black dress and hairpiece and combined all my male clothes into two boxes.

The driver took them to long-term storage, for me to someday reclaim or donate to charity, so if he didn't know I was a Chrysalis client before, he did now.

Marietta came to my suite and we had a late room-service lunch at my dining table as we used her laptop to go through ordering over two thousand dollars' worth of clothes.

The whole time, Carol was in a little window in the corner of the screen, talking to us, and sometimes she controlled the screen to show us things.

When that was done, Carol said they'd get some of them to me the next day, and the rest within about a week.

After the call ended, Marietta said she had a surprise for me.

"I waited to tell you on purpose, so you wouldn't fret about it, but that also means it's okay if it's too much of a surprise and you don't want to do it . . .

"I made you an appointment for an initial consultation with our top plastic surgeon . . . to talk about breast implants . . .

"Just so you can be well informed if and when you ever decide to consider them . . .

"And if it's too soon even to learn about them, or you never want to consider that, that's fine, I just wanted to get you a slot as quickly as possible in case—"

"Yes," I said, interrupting her.

"The only thing I don't like about my female clothes are the bra inserts, and I thought about implants while soaking in the tub last night.

"I felt like I was missing something important that implants might give me. And if that turned out to be wrong, they could always be removed later."

"Really?" Marietta said. "I was thinking this was too soon . . . or maybe I overstepped . . ."

"Marietta . . . something changed when I looked at myself wearing long, wavy hair. And again when I walked in this black dress and things yesterday. And again when I was taking a bath last night.

"On the scale of masculine vs. feminine, I really, really feel a pull to be as feminine as possible now.

"Which is scary and surprising, but it's also making me very happy so far. It's a little scary how fast my attitude has been changing, but . . . I . . . I think maybe I like myself better this way . . ."

We were still sitting side-by-side, and she gave me a hug.

"I usually tell people they can change as slowly as they want, but I don't know any reason not to change as fast as you want, as long as you're really okay with it."

"I haven't been trying to go fast, it's just been happening that way lately.

"And as for this appointment, it's just a consultation, right?" I asked. "There's no harm in learning what options are available."

"Right!" Marietta agreed.

"Oh, but . . . if that's something I'd have to pay for—"

"It's not. That's a very common service we provide at no cost. Our surgeon has an office here, but he also has another office for his private practice.

"And he's here now, and we have an appointment . . ." she looked at her phone, "in just over an hour from now."

While we were waiting, Marietta had something else to teach me that made me gasp the instant I saw them on her laptop.

Genital concealment garments—designed to cover up a micropenis or an uncommonly large clitoris, which were issues for some intersex people like me.

Some were like extra thick panties or thongs that are called gaffs that can help flatten and hide even full-sized male genitalia.

Some fit like panties, but are made out of silicone, and one variation even includes a built-in silicone tube that works as a prosthetic vagina.

There were other kinds of clips and things, but those mostly required testicles that are normal sized and fully descended—so they wouldn't work for me.

These might be desirable for three reasons: to prevent a bump from showing while wearing very tight clothes—like an evening gown or a swimsuit . . . to hide it while having sex . . . or to provide a husband with simulated vaginal sex with a wife who doesn't have a natural vagina—like might be me, if I ever decided I wanted to get married.

Not everyone who these were designed for wanted them, but for some who found their genitals embarrassing or even humiliating—definitely like me—they could be a godsend.

"How can I get those silicone panties?" I blurted out as soon as I saw them.

"I have some savings. I *really* want one! Do they come in other colors that might match me a little better?"

Marietta gave me a gentle shoulder-hug. "We have a urologist who comes when we ask her, and she has a stock with different sizes, shapes, and colors.

"Dr. Jansen will probably have a few things she can give you to start practicing with, but she'll also get your exact measurements and skin tone and order a few for you.

"She'll also teach you about how to use them, because several things about using them aren't obvious.

"I'll get the first available appointment for you," she added as she fiddled with her phone while I kept staring at the screen in amazement.

When Marietta was done, I thanked her and said, "I never even knew those existed before, but now I'm desperate for one. Is that silly?"

She paused before answering more quietly than she usually spoke, and told me that although she has a vagina, she has a micropenis instead of a clitoris, and what the difference is.

Then she also confided she wears a gaff most of the time, but when having sex with Charles she uses a half-gaff or silicone V-string style panties, because she doesn't want him to see her tiny male part.

Her phone buzzed, and after glancing at it, she said Dr. Jansen would see me at ten tomorrow.

* * *

The surgeon's office was on campus, and it was a pleasant walk as I told Marietta about my morning, including about the letter from Henry.

Dr. Harper was a tan, handsome middle-aged man, who seemed very patient, kind, and enjoyed explaining things as he examined my upper body.

I was surprised to learn that breasts of normal men and women were different in ways other than just size, and the breasts of intersex people and biological males taking estrogens could be a mix of both.

Dr. Harper was an expert at getting good implant results even with the mixed kinds, but my breasts, nipples, and areolas were completely female tissue.

The shape of my breasts, however, had been influenced by me having more male hormones than normal women.

The combination meant my cup size was just under B-cup, but I had very little fat in the lower half of them, so they didn't project forward in a rounded, teardrop way.

I was encouraged that Dr. Harper said he could make my breast shape look completely natural for a woman.

While he kept talking, I kept thinking about the odd shape issue, and became certain I wanted that fixed. *Fixed* was my term, not his.

Although I liked him, and appreciated his expertise, his endless explanations started making me impatient, once I knew I wanted to get implants plus shape correction.

As soon as he took a photo of me bare from the waist up and used his computer to show me what I could look like, I was doubly sure I wanted this.

I told him then, but he didn't seem to believe me for a while.

Once he seemed convinced I was certain, he took less time to explain things from then on.

After what seemed like a very long time, I summarized what I thought we all agreed on for me.

"Okay, so . . .

"D-cup, under the muscles, inserted from the front, repositioning but not enlarging my nipples or areolas, all sounds like the best look for my body . . .

"At the cost of more uncomfortable and longer recovery due to going under the muscles.

"The incision scars near the bottom of my breasts can be hidden even by bikinis, and in case I get married at some point, I can hide the scars before sex with sweat-resistant makeup.

"Is that right?"

Dr. Harper and Marietta exchanged glances and agreed.

"How soon could I get this done?"

"You don't want more time to think it over?" Marietta asked. "This is . . . extremely fast."

"No," I replied.

"That sounds like generally good advice, but . . . this morning while I was out and about in my old clothes, they felt foreign. Awkward.

"I'm not even close to being comfortable in women's clothes yet, but I'm going to get there fast.

"And I'm not deciding to change so much as realizing this is who I always was.

"The AI picture Mrs. Forth showed me led me to this point, and this picture of me with those breasts has convinced me this is the right thing to do, and now's the time to do it."

It took me a little longer—with Marietta's help—to convince the doctor that although I was being decisive, I wasn't being rash.

"Well . . . first thing early Monday morning, then," Dr. Harper said while fiddling with the calendar on his computer.

"No offense, Dr. Harper," I said, "but are you a morning person?"

He and Marietta laughed.

"Yes, I am. I play golf, and I prefer early morning rounds, but I'll gladly give up a round of golf for you."

*

Walking back, Marietta said, "We'll postpone you having dinner with Charles and I until you've recovered enough from surgery.

"And I texted Carol and told her to hold off on the new clothes until we get your after-surgery measurements, but she said she'd go ahead and send a few things that would work later, too.

"And forget everything I said about you having a dependent decision-making style."

"No, you were right. I just have exceptions sometimes."

"Hmm . . . well, I don't remember seeing any research on that, but offhand, that sounds like a *very* feminine trait.

"And since that took less time than I'd expected, let's stop by the salon and get you set up with some appointments . . .

"On your first appointments there, they'll start you off by applying a full set of makeup while you watch in a big mirror, and your makeup artist will explain everything she's doing and why.

"Then she'll take a set of photos of you.

"On the next appointment, they'll do it all again, but using different products and methods, again while explaining everything. Then photos again.

"They'll do that seven times, because they have seven basic looks.

"Then you'll study all your pictures and all the salon girls will help you figure out which basic looks look best on you—which may be one or any combination.

"Then . . . Michelle . . . they'll have you applying the makeup while one of them coaches you."

"You did all that?" I asked when Marietta was quiet a moment.

"I did. I started out as female-oriented, but I was terrible at makeup, and they helped a lot."

"Huh. Well, you sure look like you mastered it."

Marietta stopped walking, so I stopped and turned toward her just as she lunged forward and hugged me tight.

"Thank you for saying that . . . you have no idea how much that means to me . . ."

She pulled back and brushed at tears as we went on again.

"How fast can I get through all that?" I asked.

She laughed. "It depends on how busy they are. Why, are you in a hurry?"

"No, I . . . well . . . I guess maybe I am, but I don't know why I would be. Unless . . . maybe I'm eager to, uh . . . see . . . the final outcome . . . or something?"

"Okay . . ." Marietta said. "Well, we'll make sure they know you want to get through basic looks quickly.

"And basic looks are those you'll put on yourself, and they're often different from looks for fashion work, screen acting, or theater, and professionals will apply those kinds of makeup for you.

"Oh, and help me remember while we're there to set up appointments for skin care training, nail care, and haircare.

"It's the same process, but fewer lessons . . . first they do it while you watch, then you do it while they watch and coach.

"And they'll teach you how to use clip-in hair extensions, so when your hair gets a little longer, you can switch to that instead of a hairpiece. Then you use shorter and shorter extensions as your hair gets longer . . ."

"That all sounds very nice," I said. "And extremely generous of you and everyone.

"And will what I learn about makeup on my face work on my surgical scars, too?"

"Oh! Yes, it will, but no salon appointments until Dr. Harper okays it, so the appointments we're about to make will be tentative.

"You won't feel like it at first, anyway, but you won't be allowed to raise your hands higher than your shoulders for a while, either."

"What about feminine training?" I asked. "When does that start?"

"When you wake up after surgery on Monday, and start getting used to the weight of your new breasts.

"Posture training will be very important to keep things healthy and good-looking.

"Do you sleep face up, down, or sideways?" Marietta asked.

"All of the above," I replied.

"Not after Monday. Face up or sideways only. And not sideways until Dr. Harper clears it."

A different issue popped into my mind, so I said, "Marietta . . . my new clothes make me feel sexual, but only while I'm wearing them—at least so far. When I took a shower this morning . . . I felt like I used to.

"Suppose . . . suppose I never want to date or get married. Does that violate any of the agreements I signed? If so—"

"Oh, no, absolutely not!

"We're here to serve your needs, not the other way around.

"Manhattan Talent was founded by Raven Montague, and when it became a big success, she became very wealthy.

"As a Christian, she wanted to use that wealth to help others, and that's why she started Chrysalis and the Aurum Dating Service, not to create more wealth for herself, but to help people no one else was helping."

"Oh? So that's why Aurum welcomes intersex members?"

"Right. It's very popular with wealthy members, so it earns good profits, but even though intersex members are much less than one percent of the membership, helping intersex people find love was its primary purpose.

"And like Mrs. Montague, I think most of the people here are Christians, and share that same passion. Including me and my husband."

This time I stopped walking, and she stopped with me.

I said, “That . . . that seems kind of what people should be like . . .”

“Those who are blessed with more helping those who have less,” Marietta agreed.

“Yeah . . .” I said as I started walking again. “In my whole life, I’ve never asked for help. And I’ve never expected any . . . but you and Manhattan Talent, or Chrysalis, or both, I guess . . . I’m very grateful to you.”

Michelle Loren

Marietta called me and came over a few times over the weekend, but other than that, I was on my own most of the time.

She invited me to a church service at the campus chapel on Sunday morning, but I told her I'd think about that for future weekends.

All I had available to wear now were women's clothes, so I put them on Saturday morning to walk to Dr. Jansen's office, but I was almost too terrified to go.

I went despite my fear because I desperately wanted to get concealment panties, even though it felt like every window had people watching me take every step.

Like all the other Chrysalis doctors, Dr. Jansen was very kind, and I was amazed at how much I learned, and how well the panties concealed.

She only gave me one pair to start with, which I was wearing when I left her office, but I'd get three more in about a week, exactly my size and color.

One of them would have an artificial silicone vagina so I could see what it was like, even if I never wanted to use one.

The walk back to my suite was very different. I was much less terrified of strangers noticing me, and walking while wearing silicone panties reminded me of the first time I paced in my old room with panties and stockings.

These panties applied more pressure than regular panties, and that increased my feeling of sexuality, but Dr. Jansen said that sensation usually fades when people get used to wearing them.

Even though nothing bad happened, and my walk back to my suite felt exhilarating, it was a very stressful trip, and I spent hours in my suite decompressing and savoring the pressure.

That afternoon, I went out into the garden closest to my suite and sat on a bench. I saw a couple out for a walk, but I was very glad they didn't come near me.

On Sunday, I took several walks outside, feeling less conspicuous each time, and on my last walk, Marietta was with me.

* * *

Sometime on Monday, I started coming to after surgery, and a nurse and Marietta were right there.

"Any pain?" the nurse asked.

"Noo . . ." I mumbled. "S'fine . . ."

Without lifting my head, I looked toward my feet, and my view was blocked by my chest.

I smiled.

I wept.

Marietta lifted my hand and kissed it.

"I can feel them . . ." I slurred under my breath.

"I feel their weight . . . maybe it's the drugs . . . but I love this feeling . . ."

The nurse was in and out, but Marietta stayed with me in my private recovery room. She had my phone and game machine for me, but we just talked.

She told me about how she met Charles through the dating service, and how lucky she felt that they fell in love with each other and how that whole process played out.

Dr. Harper came by, but I don't remember anything he said. I remember he was smiling or grinning, though.

After an hour or two, the nurse raised the back of my bed about a third of the way up, and I felt the pull of gravity on my breasts change. It was a strange, delightful feeling.

I reached up to touch them, but remembered the pre-surgery instructions not to touch them for three weeks.

"You can't touch them with force," the nurse said, having noticed. "You can't push them, pull them, or squeeze them . . . but while I'm here right now, you can cup your hands over them to feel their shape."

I did, and I cried again, and thanked the nurse for her kindness and understanding.

*

After the nurse left again, Marietta asked, "Are you ready to legally become Michelle Loren, or do you want to wait longer?"

I was quiet while I thought it over.

It was a big step. A huge step.

Even bigger than surgery, to me, anyway.

Then it occurred to me that the only things I wanted to keep from my old life were my memories of my mother, my precious game machine, my phone, and my letter from Henry.

"I'm ready," I finally said.

"You can always change it back later."

"No . . ." I replied. "This is the part of me that's more than half. Despite my shriveled external genitals, it seems my ovaries won the fight for my mind.

"I don't think Leo's ever coming back."

Marietta nodded, fiddled with her phone, and held it close to my hand so all I had to do was tap a few checkboxes and squiggle my old name with my finger one last time.

"Do you drink wine?" she asked when the legal work was done.

"I've wanted to a few times, but I never have. First because my mom was an addict and I didn't want to be one, and later, also because it was an unnecessary expense."

"Okay . . . well, I brought a wine split, which is half of a normal serving. I thought we could split the split for a toast, about two swallows each, but—"

I grinned. "I'd like that. Two swallows, to say goodbye to one life and hello to a new one."

She got it out of her bag and poured it into two plastic flutes. She said, "Here's to the legal birth of Michelle Loren, and her long and happy life."

We tinked the bell ends, and she drank hers while I drank one swallow and choked and gagged, which brought the nurse running.

* * *

The next day, while I was in the sweet spot of drugged pain relief where I didn't hurt too much but also not too foggy-headed, I explained to Marietta that I'd like to try fashion and acting courses, just for fun.

And if I decided not to date or marry anyone, maybe I could work as an assistant to the fashion and acting coaches.

She was okay with that, and even thought the training and auditioning rehearsals would be a good way for me to practice thinking, appearing, and behaving as a woman.

I wouldn't be an official fashion or acting candidate without passing a regular Manhattan Talent audition interview, but Marietta could authorize me to take the classes anyway.

Although it'd be a while before I could move enough to train for modeling and acting in person, they had countless training videos I could watch.

Plus Marietta said a fashion coach and an acting coach would start visiting in a few days and getting to know me so they could recommend the videos they thought would be best suited to me.

* * *

I stayed in the recovery room until Wednesday morning, when Marietta helped me get my new measurements that she sent to Carol, and then a nurse took me back to my suite in a wheelchair while Marietta walked with us.

They pulled the covers down on my bed and helped me move from the wheelchair to the edge of the bed.

I was glancing around the room while the nurse moved the wheelchair out of the way before they were going to help ease me to the middle of the bed, and Marietta noticed me looking around.

"What are you looking for?" she asked.

"A mirror . . ." I said slowly.

They'd given me extra pain medication so it'd be having its maximum effect while I was being moved, and it made me slow thinking, slow moving, and slow talking.

"I can't see one from my bed."

"Hmm . . . no, you're right. Where would you like one?"

I lifted my hand just enough to point toward the blank wall right in front of me, then the nurse and Marietta worked together to get me centered on the bed.

That bed was a luxury model that had a remote control to raise or lower the head or my knees, which was true luxury—especially the first week after surgery, and I was extremely grateful for that.

Once I was settled, they said nurses would be in and out, but less often than in the recovery room, and Marietta said she'd be checking on me several times a day.

The nurse left, but I asked Marietta to stay a minute.

"Hairpiece, please . . . ? Not allowed for surgery for some reason . . ."

I was slurring my words badly, but she understood.

"Probably to minimize non-sterile things being nearby," Marietta said as she found it and put it on me.

"Yeah . . ." I agreed. "Didn't think that . . ."

"Oh, and do you want a free membership in the dating service? Or should I ask you later?"

"Sure, sure . . . go ahead . . ."

⁕

It wasn't great timing due to the pain drugs, but my psychologist Dr. Crowley dropped by to go over a schedule of days and times for me to meet with him over the coming weeks, and to introduce two more doctors.

One was the primary care doctor for the whole campus, who would be in charge of my regular medical care.

The other was an endocrinologist, who would be in charge of monitoring my intersex condition, and either treating me for that or coordinating treatment for it, if needed.

As long as I continued with no symptoms that needed treatment, it would mostly just be checking my hormone levels twice a year.

⁕

About half an hour after they left, there was a knock on my suite's outside door, and I hollered for them to come in, since it wasn't locked, and I assumed it was another nurse. But it wasn't.

"Hello . . ." a voice called out, followed by a man in work clothes appearing in my bedroom doorway.

"Hi . . . Michelle Loren? I brought—"

He stopped talking abruptly and stared at me a long moment.

At my face, I noticed, and only at my face.

Then he snapped out of it, cast the briefest possible glance down, where I was uncovered from the waist up except for my bandages, and he started stammering an apology as he turned away.

I pulled up the covers as fast as I could, which wasn't fast at all.

"Oh, I'm sorry!" he said in a rush. "Mrs. Sinclair sent me with your mirror. The one on casters was being used, so I'll have to mount this one to the wall, and before I bring it in from the hall, I wanted to see where you want it . . ."

"It's okay," I replied sluggishly. "I'm covered now."

He turned toward me again and I pointed as I told him where I'd like it.

Then he wheeled it in on a cart and leaned it against the wall. It was huge—full-length and wide—and it looked very heavy.

"It's not safe like this," he warned. "I've got to go out to my truck to get my tools and fasteners, so please don't go near it until I get back, okay?"

"I promise," I said with a smile, and he stared again before snapping out of it and hurrying out.

He came back and attached it to the wall, polished it, and I thanked him, and he started out with his tools, but stopped in the doorway and faced me.

"Miss Loren . . . I just have to ask . . . are you single?"

Before I could reply, he started talking fast, or at least it seemed that way to me.

"I know you're so beautiful and rich you can have any man you want and you wouldn't ever consider an ugly middle-class guy like me, but I couldn't stop myself from asking . . .

"You're just so beautiful."

With that, he spun around and rushed out.

I called out, "Wait," but I was too slow and quiet and I heard my outer door close behind him.

I have no idea what I would've said, but I wanted to say something kind to him. Especially since he was far from ugly.

*

I ignored my game machine, phone, and TV remote and just lay still, hearing haunting echoes in my mind.

"Are you single . . . ?"

"You're so beautiful . . ."

He noticed my bandaged breasts, but it was my face he stared at. My face—framed by my long hair—that prompted a man I never met before to ask me if I was single, and to tell me I was beautiful.

Then I remembered Henry, who started me down this road by telling me I was the best looking guy on our tech support team . . . which reminded me of Mrs. Forth telling me I was a good looking guy, but I was a drop-dead gorgeous woman. Which reminded me of that AI version of me with makeup.

Was I really that pretty?

I motored the back of my bed up until I was upright, and very slowly scooted to the edge of the bed and put my legs over the side—right across from the new mirror.

I gazed at myself.

I had opinions about other people's beauty, but I didn't really have one about my own.

I tried to judge my looks the same as I might judge a stranger, but something in me made that hard.

"Michelle Loren," I whispered, studying my reflection.

"I had the best feeling of my life just from pacing a few steps in panties and stockings . . .

"I have ovaries . . . hidden inside my whole life . . . flooding me all day every day with female hormones . . . shaping my face . . .

"I never felt sexual until I wore women's underwear . . .

"The first moment I had a chance to get breast implants, I jumped at it . . . I was eager for them, even though I never thought about such things until a few days ago . . ."

I felt the pull of gravity on my new breasts, but I couldn't see them clearly in the mirror anymore. I looked down at them and I noticed tears were falling onto them.

I needed to pee, but I was too tired.

I lay back down and fell asleep while all those things replayed in my mind.

Especially the way Henry had looked at me when saying goodbye, and the look on the workman's face as he stared at my face.

I woke up with the startling thought that I liked the way two men had looked at me.

No, I loved it. I wanted more of it.

It was frightening, but it was undeniable, and it was strong.

As was my need to empty my bladder, but the whole time I was taking care of that business, I was thinking about Henry and my anonymous workman.

I wanted them to look at me . . . and *desire* me . . .

I also wanted to stop feeling that way and to stop thinking about it, but my mind frequently came back to it over the rest of the week, along with all my other recent but treasured memories.

* * *

On Thursday, I stopped taking pain medication, so I hurt worse, but my mind was clearer.

Clearer, but for the rest of that week I spent as much time reminiscing and gazing at myself in the mirror as anything else.

The first time I was alone without bandages, I spent a *lot* of time looking at my new figure in the mirror, from every angle I could, wearing nothing but my silicone panties. I spent half that time crying.

I wondered if men would like my breasts. I wondered if I wanted them to, and it was scary, but . . . I did.

All my meals and snacks were brought to my suite, and I had frequent short visits from Marietta, but other than those, I played Pokémon, read on my phone, flipped channels on the huge TV screen, watched instructional videos made by Manhattan Talent and others made by Chrysalis, or . . . idly thought about my life—long past, recent past, present, and future.

When I was growing up, I was a loner, but I still had some casual friends at school and most days I saw my mom for a while.

After my mom died, I slept in an alley where a few other people did, but once I got my first call center job I was working in a room full of other people, and was able to rent a tiny room in an apartment with very annoying roommates.

Now . . . I missed being around other people.

I took a shower every couple of days, but abiding by the doctor's rules, it didn't leave me feeling very clean because I couldn't scrub.

I had to get up and walk a bit a few times a day, and a little more each day.

By the end of the week, I was going far enough to take the elevator down and go outside to enjoy the fresh air and the garden scents.

There was a lot of physical discomfort from the surgery, but I had more than enough emotional comfort from feeling the weight of my breasts to make up for it.

I loved them, so much that I often wept with joy—and I no longer cared that I cried so often.

The biggest downside I could think of was that because I couldn't raise my arms over my shoulders for a few weeks, I'd have to wait a long time to play with a lot of my new clothes.

And all that time I spent thinking and reminiscing led me to do the boldest thing I had ever done.

Call to Henry

On Friday evening, I texted Henry and asked if he had time to call me, and instead of texting me back, he called.

"Hey, Leo, how are you doing? You know we're always short-handed at work if you want to come back."

"Oh, no thanks. I, uh . . . well, first I wanted to thank you for your letter . . . and, uh . . . your suggestion that I try that Manhattan Talent app."

"Oh, really? Wow! Is that the mystery why you left us? That's great, Leo, good for you! When will we see you in a movie or something?"

"Well . . . actually, I may not ever do their kind of work. I did go to an interview, but that led in a roundabout way to me ending up at a place called Chrysalis, and—"

"Wait! What?" Henry exclaimed. "Are you joking?"

I was caught off guard by his reaction, and it took me a moment to think of a reply.

"Don't tell me you've heard of it . . ."

"What are the odds . . . ?" Henry muttered. "What are the odds?"

Then, in a normal but excited voice, he said, "I can't believe it, Leo. There must be so few people who, uh, get involved with Chrysalis, but . . .

"I'd think there must be two different places with that name, but . . . you . . . and someone else I know . . . I'm wondering how much the two of you might have in common . . . and how unlikely it is I'd know both of you if . . ."

His voice trailed off, and I asked, "So you know someone else who's a Chrysalis client?"

"Yeah, I know someone else who was a client of *a* Chrysalis . . . But I'm hesitant to say anything because I'm still thinking maybe you're hooked up with a different place with the same name, because . . . my other friend's Chrysalis . . . provides *very* unusual services."

After a pause, I quietly asked, "Tell me about your other friend, please."

Henry huffed a quick deep breath. "Okay, then, but please don't take offense if I, uh . . . well, I'll just get right into it . . .

"Will was a childhood friend . . . but he wasn't like anyone else I grew up with.

"He stayed super short, probably only weighed a hundred pounds at the end of high school . . . and I was his best friend for the simple reason that he didn't have any other friends.

"He got teased a lot, and I got into a couple of fights trying to get the teasing to stop.

"After high school, I only kept up with friends who were on social media, and he wasn't, so we lost touch until he looked me up about a year ago and wanted to get together for lunch.

"I showed up and kept an eye out for him until someone came to my table, but it wasn't Will anymore, it was Willow. A girl . . ."

"Oh," I murmured. So it *was* the same Chrysalis.

"He, or she, told me a place called Chrysalis helped him out. I mean her." He sighed heavily. "I can't keep that stuff straight.

"Anyway, after I told you about that Manhattan Talent app . . . I, uh, started thinking about you . . . like, a lot.

"And I started thinking about how good looking you are . . . and uh, wondering if you might be like Will, but I ruled that out because Will's, uh . . . body issues . . . are very rare . . .

"But then when you showed up to quit and say goodbye . . . I had two strong reactions . . .

"I didn't want to lose your friendship, and I felt that hunch again, that you might be like Will after all.

"So I wrote a quick note to give you my contact info, and . . . and I wanted to stay in touch . . . but I was also kind of afraid to . . ."

I was quiet a long time, and he said, "You still there? You mad at me?"

"Henry . . ." I said quietly, "you were right . . . about me . . ."

"Oh, wow! Are you serious?! I really have *two* friends like that? Maybe I should buy a lottery ticket.

"Sorry, I didn't mean that in an insulting way.

"So, uh, are you still in the city? You want to get together?

"I think I remember you saying you don't drink, but we could get dinner, or go for a walk in the park, or both, or something?"

"You . . . you mean like a date . . . ?" I asked.

"A date . . . ? Oh, wow, I was thinking like two friends spending some time together. Getting to know each other better, but . . . I'm open to a date, but, uh . . . this is hard to say, but uh . . ."

"My biology might be too weird for you?" I tried to finish for him.

"What? No! I don't know what your biology is, exactly, so I haven't a clue if we'd have a problem with that or not.

"No, what I mean is . . . I only date Christians . . . and I don't have sex on dates . . . I only date to get to know girls better so I can find one who will be my best friend, someone I want to spend every day with the rest of my life.

"The only iron-clad rule I have as to who that might be is they have to be a Christian, because I'm a Christian.

"Oh, and well . . . I never thought about it, but it has to be a girl, not a guy."

I was in a little state of shock and didn't reply right away, but Henry kept quiet, too.

Finally, I ventured, "I'm not a Christian, but I could become one. Would that be good enough?

"And . . . I'm biologically part male and part female . . . so would that rule me in or out?"

"Wow . . . Leo, I've always definitely wanted a wife, not a husband . . . but until I met Willow, I didn't even know half and half existed—I mean intersex . . . is that the right term? And I know it's not exactly half and half . . ."

He was quiet again, and I whispered, "Henry . . . I'm not Leo anymore. That's how I was raised, but I figured out the female parts of me are more than half, so . . . now . . . I'm . . . Michelle Loren . . ."

"Michelle Loren . . ." Henry said slowly and warmly.

"That may be the most beautiful name I've ever heard . . . but I've thought of a problem for us . . . because I met Leo first . . .

"When I look at you from now on . . . it might be a big problem for me if my brain sees you as Leo and not as Michelle. Although . . . maybe that wouldn't be the case . . . because your face was always so . . . so . . . good-looking . . ."

I was anxious for Henry to accept how I'd been changing, and I said, "You were right about Chrysalis, too.

"I went there, and they . . . they've been extremely kind and helpful, and the first day . . . they showed me a picture of a beautiful young woman.

"I didn't recognize myself at first, but it was me, with long hair and makeup.

"And now . . . they're teaching me how to, uh, look like that in real life, and to develop behaviors and manners to match."

"No kidding? Wow, Michelle, that's . . . kind of exciting . . . I'm kind of eager to see if, uh, that side of things could work out for us, but, uh . . . about the issue of Christianity . . .

"Anyone can become a cultural Christian just by saying they are and adopting a few outward Christian appearances, like going to church or celebrating Christmas, but I can only marry a spiritual Christian."

"Oh . . . ? Well . . . do you think I might be able to do that?"

"You definitely could, but it will cost you your life, and not many people are willing to pay that price.

"Seriously. You can only become a spiritual Christian by giving your whole life to God. It's absolutely worth it, but you can't really know that ahead of time.

"You have to have enough faith in God to be willing to give your life completely to him."

We were both quiet again, until Henry said, "Would you like to meet me to talk about that more? And for us to get to know each other better besides that?"

This time we were both quiet, but Henry just waited for me to say something.

"Henry . . . I had surgery recently . . . breast implants . . . and it took a lot of mental energy out of me just to text you . . . and now I'm really tired and it's getting hard for me to think . . ."

He didn't interrupt and waited for me to go on.

"I'd like to meet with you for all the reasons you said . . . but I'm not in the city and I won't be able to move around much for weeks.

"I won't be fully healed for months. I don't know what to do."

"How about this?" Henry said. "I'll call you in either one month or two months, you choose."

"One month, please," I said without hesitation.

"Okay. That's a big relief, 'cause if you waffled on that and said something indefinite like let's just wait and see, I'd have thought you didn't really want to see me again and were just too polite to say so."

Thinking was getting harder by the moment, but I managed to say something like, "Henry . . . the note you gave me is one of my most treasured possessions, and I don't have many.

"And . . . I guess you're my best male friend for the same reason you were Will's best friend. I don't want to lose your friendship, and I don't want to disappoint you."

"That means a lot to me, Michelle. And it means a lot that you trusted me enough to tell me everything you have tonight, and I want you to know I won't tell anyone else. Okay?"

"Okay, Henry. Thank you."

"You're welcome, Michelle. You're very welcome."

After we hung up, I wondered if Willow was a Christian, and if Henry thought she's attractive.

Not long after that, I drifted off to sleep for the night with three new phrases echoing in my thoughts:

"Your face was always so, so good-looking."

"It will cost you your life."

But mostly it was hearing the way Henry said my new name.

Dating App

That Saturday morning, I had a text waiting from Marietta asking why I hadn't ever logged into the Aurum Dating Service app.

Well, that was because I hadn't wanted to when she first told me about it, and then I'd forgotten all about it.

I was a little tired of my game machine, training videos, and browsing my favorite Internet sites, so I decided to download the app and look at it before replying to Marietta.

As soon as I opened up the app I saw I had numerous notifications waiting, but I ignored those at first because I was distracted by a link, labeled: "Prime Member Interest: 33."

I clicked it and it opened to a new page.

ADS prime members interested: 33
Grouped by Net Worth:
$10-19M: 18 members
$20-29M: 7 members
$30-39M: 1 member
$40-49M: 3 members
$50-75M: 1 member
$76-100M: 1 member
> $100M: 2 members

That surprised me, because I was sure Marietta had said they had a lot of prime members, and this wasn't a lot. Although the levels of wealth were impressive—if they were real.

I wanted to text Marietta and ask her to come see me, and started thinking of what I wanted to write, but that issue was solved when she walked in.

"Michelle? What's wrong?" she asked with mild concern as soon as she saw me.

"The dating service only has thirty-three prime members?" I asked, trying not to sound contrary.

"No, there are several thousand. Where'd you get thirty-three from?

Without a word, I turned my phone and held it for her to see.

She glanced at it and smiled.

"Dear . . . that's how many have expressed interest in *you*, specifically. And that number will keep going up for a while as others get around to checking their notifications."

That stunned me, and I looked at the list again.

"C-can . . . can this be right . . . ?"

"Sure. The count's been slowly going up since I put you in the system a few days ago. Plus a big jump this morning because of your new status."

I shook my head. "What new status?"

Marietta grinned.

"That's what I came to tell you."

She told me what to tap on in the Manhattan Talent app . . . to see that I was now qualified for advanced auditions for both fashion and acting.

"When I created your dating app account," Marietta said, "I set your sex as intersex, and the interest started as soon as I turned it on.

"This morning, I remembered to change your audition profile from male to female.

“We’re allowed to make factual corrections, and when I did that, the system rated you as passing the photo audition for both fashion and acting. Then—”

“Wait . . .” I interrupted, “you mean if I’d put my sex as female at the start I would’ve been chosen for fashion and acting?”

Marietta looked sympathetic. “I think so . . . it appears our AI thinks your face is exceptionally suitable as a female model, but not as a male model . . .”

“Well . . .” I sighed, “I guess that reinforces the idea that I’m more woman than man . . .

“But I never passed the second part of the in-person interview.”

“Yes, you did.” Marietta said happily. “When you talked to the fashion and acting coaches, that counted—they recommended you.”

“So when your Manhattan Talent account designated you this morning as both a fashion and acting candidate, that got automatically sent to your Aurum profile.

“That obviously had a favorable influence on some of our dating clients, even though it shouldn’t.

“Candidates pursuing fashion or acting can make poor romantic partners, because they usually devote themselves to their career instead of to their spouse.

“But that’s when the number of interested clients jumped up some. The slow growth comes because as more time goes by, more clients get around to reviewing new candidates.

“Oh, and since you haven’t been paying attention to it, I’ll also mention that they can see a new AI image of you, modified from the makeup and long hair headshot, to a mid-shot showing you from the waist up, and including your new AI-imagined breasts. Fully clothed, of course.”

“What?!”

She told me what to tap to pull it up to see for myself, and once again . . . it was really hard to believe that was me.

I sighed. "So I can do fashion or acting—maybe—but I shouldn't, if I want romance?"

"Correct . . . in my opinion. Most of our candidates are here for fashion or acting, and some will sacrifice everything else for that.

"And the income Manhattan Talent earns by acting as their agents is a major source of income for the company. Even more when companies rent our studios to do shoots with our models.

"For fashion models or actors, Manhattan Talent can provide training to help them audition well and perform well, and if they do well enough, the company will get gigs for them.

"The company's commission is fifteen percent, and if they have a manager, they take another ten percent, but the model or actor's share often reaches six figures a year.

"When you're doing those gigs, though, it's extremely demanding work, often with unsavory people. Long, hard hours, which drives many people in those industries to use drugs to try to keep up.

"We do what we can to protect our models and actors, and we recommend good managers, but there's only so much we can do."

I shivered.

"That killed my mom. The drugs and alcohol, I mean, not the jobs . . ."

Marietta nodded solemnly, and I told her something I'd never told another soul.

"My mother was a prostitute . . . I never knew my father, because she didn't know who he was . . ."

Her eyes watered and she swallowed hard. "I'm very glad she gave birth to you . . . and that you survived all that . . ."

"Most of my life," I said, "I never cared much whether I lived or died. I just marched along. Sometimes mom wouldn't be home for a couple of days, and it got so that every time she went out, I was afraid she might never come back.

"When she died, I wanted to die for a while after that, but I didn't, so I just . . . tried to survive. I lived on the streets for a while, and that was terrifying.

"But now . . . I feel different about my life than I ever have before—and not because of wealthy potential suitors or high-paying lousy jobs.

"Now I feel happy to be me . . . just to be alive, as me."

"Wow . . ." Marietta said. "You've had a really remarkable life so far . . . I don't work with our models and actors, but my impression is that most don't come from such a hard background.

"The backgrounds of our Chrysalis clients is all over the map, however, and your story is definitely on the extremely hard side . . .

"But now let me see you walk a little. Let's take the elevator down and go outside to sit on a bench. The temperature's perfect, with a light breeze."

"Okay. But I'm not going to race you."

*

We made it and sat down on a cushioned bench.

"Hey, Marietta, I've got another question for you. Those prime members interested in dating me . . . how much do they know about me?"

"I know you didn't bring your phone with you," Marietta said, "but there's a way for you to see that in the app. You go to your profile and there's a link to View as Prime Member.

"Your training schedule has me going over that in detail with you next week, but since you're asking now, I'll tell you what I can from memory . . .

"The first thing they saw was your first AI image, a 'Female seeking Male' category tag, a placeholder name, like Member A100 or something like that, and a five-year age range.

"If they opened your profile, they could see that you have OT syndrome, the second AI image from your waist up, and they may assume the breasts are implants.

"By the way, Aurum goes to great lengths to filter out bad guys from our service.

"They can't buy their way in no matter how rich they are if they don't pass our requirements.

"My main job is as a senior certified counselor for Chrysalis, but I also work for Aurum, on their member requirements committee, and we look out for our members like they were our dear brothers or sisters. Like how I feel about you."

I was quiet a long time thinking about all that, then asked, "Do they know I don't have a vagina?"

"They may know you probably don't, because about ninety percent of OT people don't, and their ADS dating coach should point that out to them. Although there's some lag time between a prime member tagging your profile and the next time their coach talks to them."

"So . . . the ones who already know I probably can't have children . . . they're interested anyway? Why don't they want children?

"Oh, and what about sex . . . ?

"Yes, if they stay interested in you, then they're okay with not having natural children with you. They might be open to adoption, or, if they're divorced, they may already have children.

"As for sex, many men want it every way they can get it, but you can filter your profile to whatever methods you're okay with, and the matchmaking algorithm will apply that.

"So that you can make informed choices, you'll have extensive lessons on sex with hands, mouth, anus, and toys. For you, that includes the option of silicone panties with a built-in prosthetic vagina."

"Do I have to do the lessons on anal sex?" I asked. "I'm not sure I want to have sex at all, but I hate that idea especially."

"It's not mandatory, but are you aware that it's possible to do it so that it's moral, clean, safe, and fun for both him and you?"

"That's a little hard to believe," I replied, "but I've been learning lots of things I couldn't have believed a few weeks ago.

"Oh . . . but are any of these guys gay, and trying to hide that behind a feminine-looking wife?"

"We've done extensive analysis of our prime membership base," Marietta said, "and they have different reasons that fall into several clusters . . . and none of those reasons are being a closeted homosexual, which we filter out.

"And gay guys don't need ADS, because there're plenty of other dating sites that are specialized for them.

"Typically, prime members—almost all men—have assistants sign them up on multiple dating services in addition to ours, and even on ADS they're searching among fully biological women in addition to our intersex members.

"The biggest reason prime members include ADS in addition to others is the rigorous admissions process for standard members.

"And among the clusters who are interested in intersex women, the largest is guys who have poor social skills or marginal physical appeal.

"They're not bad looking, but some aren't great looking—with a few very handsome exceptions.

"This group, more than anything else, wants someone who will appreciate them for who they are, rather than for their wealth.

"They know that they can't hide their wealth, and that it enhances their overall appeal, and they may even flaunt it . . .

"But they think—because we tell them so—that intersex people have often been marginalized and overlooked.

"They think two people who are keenly aware of their own flaws are more likely to be accepting of flaws in each other as romantic partners. And our history proves that's generally true."

"Wow . . ." I muttered as I adjusted my position on the cushioned bench. "I like that . . . but what's another group?"

"The next largest group—and all these groups overlap some—is guys who've had good sex and bad sex, and want to make sure they don't get stuck having bad sex again.

"With Aurum, they'll know before they marry one of our members that you're both completely matched on what you want when it comes to physical satisfaction."

"Um . . . well . . . I've never had sex. How can I know if I'd be any good at it?"

"You'll have a lot of training for that. You'll know how to enjoy it yourself and how to ensure they enjoy it."

"Ouch," I said as I shifted my position to try to ease the weight of my breasts becoming more uncomfortable on my incision spots.

"I have some questions about that, but first I'd like to know what the other types of clients are."

"Let's get you back to bed," she said, helping me up. "Those two groups cover almost everyone, and all the rest are more niche and in addition to one or both of the first two, and we'll cover them next week."

"Okay . . . but give me an example . . . after we get back to my suite."

*

"Charity," she resumed a few minutes later. "Some of our clients don't care if they have sex with a normal woman or an intersex woman, but they think it's an act of kindness to partner with an intersex woman who they presume has fewer romantic chances.

"When we detected that trait, our first impulse was to exclude them, but then we studied it and discovered those men were usually excellent husbands, so they're still allowed. And remember, that trait is usually in addition to one or more other traits."

"Another, please," I asked as I eased into bed.

Marietta sighed, but with a smile. "Some see intersex women as the ultimate trophy wife."

I laughed, and it hurt.

"Seriously, usually in addition to other reasons, they think intersex is cool simply because you're so rare."

"Well . . . dang," I said.

"Listen, I have to be in our chapel service tomorrow from ten to noon, but I'll come check on you before and after.

"You're always welcome there except when it's against doctor's orders for you to be out of bed that long, which it is tomorrow."

"Oh . . ." I replied. "Yeah . . . I've never been to church, and no one's ever invited me before you did last week."

"In that case, fear of the unknown might bother you, so if you'd like, tomorrow afternoon I'll bring my laptop and we can watch a video of a church service together, and we can pause every time you want me to explain something."

"I'd like that very much," I said. "I've very recently developed an interest in church. Well, something related to that."

* * *

That evening Marietta called.

"Hey. Still okay?" she asked.

"I'm busy playing Pokémon and mourning not being able to soak in a hot bath for the first *month* after my surgery. I seriously undervalued that cost of getting the surgery done."

She laughed and asked if I minded talking a few minutes, and of course I didn't mind.

"I want to make sure you don't feel pressured to study our lessons on anal sex," she said.

"Thanks! I really appreciate that. But . . . maybe I could try the first lesson . . . then decide if I want to see the next one?"

"Sure! That sounds like a very good idea."

"Thanks, Marietta. I guess you're glad you don't have to deal with that, since you can do it the normal way."

She was quiet long enough that I started to wonder if I said something wrong.

"Charles and I do it the normal way most of the time . . ." she paused, then continued, "but sometimes we don't."

That was very surprising news, and I appreciated her being willing to confide that to me, but I didn't know what to say after that, so we ended the call with me thanking her for "giving me something to think about."

At bedtime, I definitely didn't want my mind thinking about that as I tried to go to sleep, but fortunately, the only thing from the day's conversations that crept into my echoes was "trophy wife."

Invitation

On Sunday, I enjoyed watching the church service video with Marietta, especially with all her commentary during and after.

I almost asked her about becoming a spiritual Christian, but I decided to wait until after I attended at least one chapel service in person.

My only training the week after my surgery was mostly learning what to expect, watching videos, two sessions with Dr. Crowley by video call on my phone, and Marietta answering my endless questions.

The week after that, I was on a pretty busy schedule, although it didn't include anything that needed me to raise my hands above my shoulders.

I only started my lessons at the salon late that second week, when the ladies were applying my makeup and I was only watching.

My first day in the salon, the girls all complimented my breasts, and I was surprised I wasn't horribly embarrassed.

They took pictures of me with each of their seven basic looks, and they and Marietta agreed with my choice of the one that made me look most like the AI image Mrs. Forth had shown me when it flipped my world upside down.

The week after that I got to start putting it on myself, and I was pretty poor at it at first, but I was really good in a week or two.

I was surprised at how time-consuming it could be, but I really enjoyed it . . . and I began to have faint longings to have someone to look pretty for.

I usually had at least two sessions a day with Marietta, which were usually about feminine mannerisms, behavior, and sexuality, and two a week with Dr. Crowley, the psychologist.

I was also learning to socialize as a woman with other residents and the staff, and I was quickly becoming friends with all of them . . . and that *never* happened before in my whole life.

About two weeks after my surgery, I started having dinner with Marietta and her husband Charles, once every two or three days.

It was a great chance to practice a kind of socializing I had zero experience with, and it gave me a great opportunity to wear my beautiful clothes—more and more of them as I was allowed to move my arms more.

*

From the beginning of my time at Chrysalis, something inside was often driving me to binge-watch training videos, and I was learning more and faster than I'd ever learned anything.

But there was one major disruption to my ability to concentrate for a while.

* * *

A few days before I expected Henry to call on his one-month follow-up, I texted him again, asking him to call me when he had time. He called a little late that evening.

"Hi, Michelle! How are you?" he asked happily. "I just got home from work."

"I'm feeling great compared to how I felt when I asked you to call last time. I've wanted to call you many times since last time, but . . . well . . . I guess I was a little shy, and uh—"

"Me, too," Henry said. "My main excuse for not calling before is that I've been busier than ever, but I also thought you might want to stay focused on your studies—you know, no distractions.

"And I didn't know your schedule, or how busy you are . . ."

"Oh . . . well . . . uh, I'm at Chrysalis in the Hamptons, and—"

"You're in the Hamptons? Wow! Is that where you've been since you left?"

"It is, and it's beautiful here. It's an estate owned by Manhattan Talent, and it's like a luxury resort. There're no entertainment options here, but it's very beautiful."

"Oh, nice! I'm happy for you, Michelle! That sounds great."

"Well, I was wondering . . ."

I took a quick deep breath to renew my resolve.

"If there's any chance you might enjoy spending one of your precious days off taking the train up here to visit me for a few hours."

I didn't mention that I had a surprise I wanted to give him in person.

He didn't reply right away, and every second he waited, my anxiety doubled.

"I want to drop everything and come right away," he said, removing my anxiety completely, but then replacing it with great disappointment.

"But I've got a couple of problems . . . the reason I've been busier than ever is because I got a promotion at work. I'm a manager now—"

"Oh, Henry, that's wonderful!" I exclaimed.

"Well, yes and no. I'm finally getting some value out of my business degree again, and I'm earning twice as much money now, but it's also twice as many hours. I'm salaried, and I have almost no free time . . .

"I can schedule some time off, but I've already done that to go to a cousin's wedding in about a month.

"I promised to be a groomsman and everything, so I feel committed to that . . . and I already know my boss won't like me taking more time off anytime soon . . ."

His voice trailed off, and after he stayed quiet, I ventured, "So, it might be several months at the soonest before you could come see me? And maybe a lot longer than that?"

He sighed heavily. "I thought my promotion was a step up . . . but now it seems like it's an anchor. I really want to come see you very soon, but it seems like I've made that impossible."

We chatted a few more minutes with me trying to sound happy while my heart was breaking, but I couldn't keep it up.

"Henry . . . I love listening to your voice, but I have to go. I'm sorry, but . . . I'm about to start crying, and I don't want you to hear me do that."

Maybe I shouldn't have told him that, because it upset him, but I said it because I didn't want him to imagine that the reason I was ending our call abruptly was because I was angry or disappointed in him.

We said an awkward goodbye, and when the line went dead, I felt lonelier than I ever had before.

Training

I wasn't just learning a lot the first month, I was also changing—a lot.

One of the biggest changes was what had once been a repugnant idea—dating or kissing a man—had evolved through me being open to it, to an inkling of interest, all the way to desire.

It seemed my feminine nature had swept aside all remnants of my former self-image.

I was born to be a woman—or at least mostly woman—and I had come very close to embracing everything that included.

And I was certain now that I was going to keep racing down that path as far as I was capable of going.

Which presented a major question: Should I give up a possible career in modeling or acting to pursue romance?

Marietta and Dr. Crowley advised me to pursue both, with an expectation that if I found true love, I'd easily be able to give up a so-far non-existent career.

And if romance didn't come to me, I might have a good career to support myself.

I'd told Dr. Crowley—but not Marietta for some unknown reason—that Henry was the leading character in more and more of my dreams.

And the doc had warned me that sometimes people set their desires on something unattainable as a defense mechanism against something stressful.

Could I be setting my heart on Henry because he was unattainable, and by doing that, it blocked me from the stressful idea of pursuing some of the wealthy members of Aurum?

If I was, so far I was powerless to stop it, even with the doctor's help.

On the other hand, the doctor pointed out that I already knew Henry and I both liked each other and we had some shared history.

Working in the same call center wasn't much history together, but it was more than I had with any of the rich guys in Aurum.

Plus my phone call with Henry . . . where I'd learned he'd fought bullies to protect a smaller guy. Plus . . . I'd worked with lots of other guys, and had male roommates, and Henry was the only guy I was now attracted to.

Because . . . he was kind. He was kind to everyone, yes, but . . . I wasn't just aware of his kindness, I *felt* his kindness toward me.

And . . . I just realized . . . I was attracted to him because he's good-looking.

Me. I was attracted to Henry. Sexually.

Because he's good-looking.

What had been impossible had happened.

But would Henry ever want me with my less than fully female body?

I could never be a normal wife for him. If we got married, I'd be robbing him of a normal life.

And if I could earn a lot of money in modeling or acting or marry Henry . . . what should I do?

* * *

Early in my second month at Chrysalis, Marietta sat with me to go through a dating preferences profile, similar to what all prime members had to complete.

She warned me that once I submitted mine, their computer would compare my preferences with all the prime member preferences.

When that happened, the number of members interested in me would probably drop a lot because they'd be mismatches based on what we all wanted, needed, were willing to accept, and weren't willing to accept.

Obviously, the narrower I set my preferences, the fewer matches would remain, but Marietta and Dr. Crowley advised me to make my choices based on what kind of man I could be happy with " 'til death do us part."

After I submitted my preferences, those members who were still matches, if any, would find out my first name, and I could see theirs.

Marietta also told me that even prime members are required to do independent-study training, and take proctored exams to prove they were really learning.

A lot of their training was basic things covered by many premarital training courses, but with lots of things that were more advanced about how to be a good husband.

I *loved* my classes on how to be a good wife, and I hoped their parallel lessons were as good as mine were.

I was also told that I should expect a hand-written letter from each of the ones who were still interested in me, as that was a requirement to have a chance to date me.

And for me, it would reveal some of their social skills and writing skills, whether good or bad.

If the letters were poor, that would be a very bad sign, because they had counselors who were trying to teach them how to write appealing letters to introduce themselves to me.

Even after I had all my preferences set, I was very reluctant to submit them, so I procrastinated a few days, but eventually I did it.

After the computer matching, which only took a few seconds, I had eight possible suitors left.

Over the next couple of weeks, I got eight letters. Seven of them were all nice, but very similar, and focused on telling me about themselves, which seemed appropriate.

The exception was from Roger, and he spent a lot of his letter telling me how much he'd like to get to know me and how he hoped we'd find ways we could enjoy spending time together.

For each of them, I wrote a short note thanking them for their letter, but I was noncommittal about anything else.

The next step up the ladder of romance, if I wanted to take it, was to decide if I wanted to try dating.

I was in no hurry to make that choice, and my studies helped me postpone a decision about it.

And the longer I waited, the better prepared I'd be for dating based on much of what I was learning.

*

Also early in my second month, on a post-op checkup, Dr. Harper pierced my earlobes and gave me my first pair of earrings—diamond and sterling silver studs.

For a while after getting them, every time I looked at myself in a mirror, those diamonds took all my attention.

Right after that, Marietta told me I had a surprise coming, but refused to tell me what it was.

A few days later, Carol from the clothing store came to Chrysalis, and stopped by to see me . . . and showed me a lot of beautiful jewelry.

Marietta had never said anything about me being given jewelry, but after the full wardrobe they'd given me, I was wondering about that while Carol was showing it all to me, one thing at a time.

After showing me everything, Carol asked me to guess how much it all cost. I had no clue.

"Does twenty thousand dollars sound about right?" she asked when I was too intimidated to guess.

"Yeah," I replied. "I wouldn't have been surprised if you'd said a lot more than that."

"It's all three hundred dollars," she stated. "It's costume jewelry. This gold ring is actually plastic."

I blinked. Then I gazed at her, waiting for a punchline.

"Here's a very important lesson, Michelle.

"You thought all this was precious metals and gemstones because I brought it, and you associate me with a very elite and expensive clothing shop. The actual price doesn't matter as much as the context.

"If you behave like a kind but sophisticated woman with good posture, people will assume you're wealthy."

The man who installed the big mirror in my suite flashed through my mind. Something had made him assume I was rich . . . was it just because I was a resident here?

"This is all for you to keep and enjoy," Carol continued, "and if you present yourself well, people will assume it's all expensive.

"If you're fortunate enough to get expensive pieces in the future, you can start wearing those and retire these . . . but always remember that these are an object lesson.

"Present yourself as classy, and people will accept you as classy."

*

My first few training sessions with Marietta on feminine attractiveness had been eye-opening, and it turned out they were all like that.

Many of them were specifically for intersex women, to help us deal with our biological handicaps, but I had at least one thing in my favor . . .

Marietta said I was extremely fortunate with my face, which would help compensate for how I appeared when undressed in front of a husband.

For example, she explained that cognitive testing had been done with men wearing a helmet of sensors, which showed how their brains react to many different traits of femininity and masculinity.

In that and other studies, most heterosexual men are attracted to anything and everything feminine.

Since my genitalia isn't feminine, I learned I can compensate by emphasizing the feminine traits I did have, and were developing.

I wouldn't be able to satisfy most men due to my mixed up genes, but there were some who could be attracted to me despite that, and I had a list of eight of them who were specifically attracted to me!

All that gave me a lot to think about, and if what I'd been learning was true . . .

I had the face, the breasts, and the figure, and I was in the process of gaining the behavior, attitudes, mannerisms, and everything else to make me as feminine as any woman alive—for things that were under my control.

And week after week, I was increasingly savoring the idea of being desirable to men . . . I was seeing it in some of the male instructors and fellow modeling and acting students.

It was flattering, and I liked that feeling.

*

Distinct from lessons on feminine attractiveness were lessons called feminine enthusiasm—or more precisely, feminine sexual enthusiasm.

It was partly about how to perform sexual techniques, but mostly about attitude, and all of it was oriented toward keeping both my husband and myself sexually and emotionally satisfied.

The reason the course was called enthusiasm despite involving other things was because a husband's and a wife's enthusiasm for sex outweighed all other factors combined for sexual fulfillment, and sexual fulfillment was a key part of emotional fulfillment for most people.

At first, I wasn't interested, but I was willing to go through the lessons because I figured there wouldn't be much too it. Wow, was I wrong—on two counts.

One, there's been an overwhelming amount of research about such things, and two . . .

I was changing.

A wind was blowing through my mind, taking all my old ways of looking at the world and myself, and leaving behind only one thing: A woman.

A genetically mutated woman, but a woman nonetheless.

I was both learning what it means to be a woman, and even more to my surprise, I was embracing it.

That was hard to believe at first, but then I had an insight where my old life—based on a misunderstanding of my body—was like a piece of gravel, and my new life was like a flawless diamond turning in the sunlight.

Gravel was fine for some purposes, but why be gravel when I was born to be a diamond?

My favorite parts of this training so far were the power of enthusiasm, the idea to engage all five senses, and "reciprocal interactions."

Those lessons taught me that enthusiasm works so well, it even works when it's faked, and it even works when the other person knows it's faked!

I didn't believe that at first, and Marietta told me she didn't either when she first learned about that, but she said she and Charles had experimented with it on different occasions, when one of them was too tired to be genuinely enthusiastic, but not too tired to pretend—and it worked just like the researchers described!

Lessons on engaging all five senses taught me:

1. different ways to touch and to touch everywhere;
2. different ways to provide visual stimulation, including body language and eye contact;
3. tasting is through kissing—mouth to mouth frequently, oral sex often, but everywhere else sometimes, too;
4. different ways to provide audio stimulation, mostly through different kinds of moans and words with different intensities, and different kinds of background music; and
5. different kinds of scents.

Lessons on reciprocal interactions during sex also covered a lot of ground, including synced and counter-synced movements and taking turns on vigorous movements.

I didn't have a husband and didn't know if I ever would, but sometimes as I reflected on everything I was learning, I thought if I ever did, I'd be a dynamo in bed.

And even if I never got married, one of my acting coaches told me everything I was learning, including about sex, would help me better portray a wider variety of characters.

* * *

Towards the end of my first month at Chrysalis, I'd started in-person modeling and acting lessons in addition to ever more video lessons.

The purpose of the in-person lessons was to coach me for the possibility of live Manhattan Talent professional auditions, and week-by-week I was enjoying them more and more.

My main coaches were a Manhattan Talent fashion photographer who was their main trainer for that, another was a retired theater director, and another was an accomplished movie director.

The movie director taught what they called screen acting, which covers movies and TV.

To my surprise, they all said I was very good for a beginner, and Marietta gave me a copy of their written reports after I completed my second stages of their training.

They rated me as above average in confidence and presence, professionalism and work ethic, adaptability and versatility, passion and enthusiasm, emotional intelligence and interpersonal skills, and physical stamina and presentation.

It also explained what all that meant.

Before I read it, I thought my only strength was in mimicking what they showed me.

They must have been sincere, though, because they decided to set up professional auditions for me for all three disciplines in one day at the Manhattan Talent studios in NYC.

My coaches wouldn't be allowed to attend, and Marietta wasn't available to drive me.

They would've lent me a car, but I didn't have a driver's license, so they assigned a staffer to take me, wait for me, and bring me back—and it was the same chatty driver who had taken me to the city to get my old clothes and say goodbye at work.

If the driver knew he'd driven me before as Leo, he didn't let on.

I'd hoped I'd be able to see Henry while I was in town, but I was told I'd be very busy every minute and I'd be exhausted by the end of the day.

And they were right about all that, and I think the busyness helped, because I never got nervous at all.

In fact, it was a lot of fun, even when I was tired.

Mrs. Forth came by once to say hello and ask how things were going, but I suspected she might know more about how things were going with me than I did.

She still intimidated me, but to my surprise I acted as I'd been trained, and gave a polite, professional reply that everything was going very well, and I thanked her for all her help.

I got back to Chrysalis late that evening and all my training went back to normal.

* * *

About a week later, Marietta sat me down with a serious look on her face.

"You passed all three of your professional auditions, Michelle . . . they love your looks and your skills."

She paused, I guessed for me to say something, but I was too stunned.

"So," she finally said, "the world's your footstool . . . if you want it, but you have to pick one and only one.

"The agency won't let you do more than one—not to start with. So, have you decided if you have a preference? You can—"

"Screen-acting," I replied.

"At first I thought I liked that better because I liked Mr. Bennett better, but it's not just that . . . I like everything about screen acting better."

"Okay, then. Dr. Harper will probably clear you for acting work at about five months post-surgery, as long as you and the people hiring you agree to certain conditions."

"And he's always said I'd be okay for unlimited activities at twelve months," I said.

"If everything has gone well, yes," Marietta agreed.

"And speaking of going well . . . you have your first job offer.

"Your screen acting coach, Jim Bennett, told me that if you go down this road, he wants to offer you a supporting role in a movie he has in pre-production.

"Shooting is expected to start early next year."

"I'm sorry . . . say that again . . ."

"You have an offer for your first acting job."

I took a deep breath and let it out slowly as I shook my head.

"Maybe . . . maybe I never actually thought this would work . . . I don't know what to think . . . or feel . . ."

"Well," Marietta assured me, "you don't have to do any of that, but if you do, Jim is a great guy for you to start with.

"He'll take care of you as if you were his daughter—he has two, by the way—and he has a good track record as a movie producer and director."

"And I like him a lot . . ." I said, "but I think I need to spend some time thinking about this a lot more seriously than I have up to now."

"That can't hurt," she agreed. "Oh, and there's one thing in particular you especially need to consider . . . your biography.

"Chrysalis clients have always preferred to keep their intersexuality private, except with the Aurum dating service. And Aurum's prime members also prefer that be kept private . . .

"Fashion models and actresses, however, have fans, and those fans want to know everything about their celebrity's background. *Everything.*

"You're rare because you have OT syndrome.

"You're doubly rare because you're extraordinarily beautiful and talented at both fashion and acting. That makes you unique. And gives you a big decision to make."

"So . . ." I thought out loud, "I need to decide if I'm willing for strangers to know about my mom and that I'm intersex?"

"Yeah, I think so.

"I'll talk to Mrs. Forth about this, and you should talk to Dr. Crowley about it.

"If you become a model or actress, you can try to keep your background secret, and it might work, but the more famous you get, the harder reporters will work for every detail they can dig up.

"Your male to female name change is a public record, and your face is distinctive enough that people you've worked with might recognize you and make posts on social media . . ."

I sighed. "And the rich guys should know if that's a possibility before I start dating them."

"They're aware of your pursuit of fashion and acting, and now that you're starting work on screen, their coaches should point that out to them," Marietta said.

"Double-checking that's one of the things I need to discuss with Mrs. Forth."

"Oh. Well, the odds of me becoming famous are near non-existent, so that helps."

Marietta shook her head.

"You're underestimating how beautiful you are.

"In *two* industries where that's a premium asset."

I might be underestimating a little, but I figured she might be overestimating a lot.

First Date

I continued training and my body continued to heal from surgery, but it all felt different somehow.

Dr. Crowley started helping me learn how to deal with success in mentally healthy ways, and I started video lessons on that, too.

On dealing with success.

Because . . . I was having some success . . . as an actress . . . as a female!

*

It was up to me to decide if or when I'd try dating, and just between me, Marietta, and Dr. Crowley, I set a tentative goal of trying a first date with a rich guy. And my new openness to dating was due to two events.

One was that I was interested in going on a date with Henry, and if I was going to do that, it seemed like I ought to at least give the rich guys a chance since their fees helped fund Chrysalis.

The other was when I was shocked out of my sleep around 4 a.m., due to having a sex dream that was so extremely vivid and intense that I woke up shaking, gasping, and sweaty.

And in it . . . I was a happy wife . . . although my husband was indistinct, which seemed fine while I was dreaming, but was disappointing after I woke up.

I took a warm shower just to rinse the sweat off, and I thought about this event.

I decided no matter how embarrassing it was, I'd tell Marietta and Dr. Crowley and see what they had to say about it, but I suspected—and hoped—that this was a sign that maybe my mind and body were ready . . . for me to actually be a wife.

Oh, and Marietta told me that before I dated anyone on Aurum, she'd personally tell that member's dating coach about the possibility of my intersexuality becoming public knowledge, and the coach would tell the member.

About two weeks later I got a text from Henry.

"Talked things over with my boss, my cousin and his fiancée, and my family. I'm not going to their wedding.

"As for work, I've been having to work on a lot of supposed days off, but they promised me I can come see you on any Tuesday if I tell them in advance.

"Could you have a visitor on a weekday? If a Tuesday won't work, tell me any day that will work for you and I'll try to make it work. Instead of taking the train, I'll rent a car for the day."

I replied immediately, "!!! I'll have to check with a lot of people, but I'll let you know as soon as I find out! !!!"

I called Marietta first, and she delighted me by telling me to tell Henry his first available Tuesday would be fine, and that she would take care of notifying all my instructors and Dr. Crowley.

As soon as I got off the phone with Marietta, I tried calling Henry, and he answered after four or five rings. I told him the good news, and he sounded really excited. I know I was.

Then he got serious, and asked, "So . . . Michelle . . . are you . . . I don't know how to ask this tactfully, so forgive me if I'm too blunt, but . . . are you adjusting to things?

"Are you glad you started this? Are you happy?"

“Henry, everything’s going far better than I ever could have imagined.”

I didn’t say it, but that included him wanting to come see me.

He was happy with my answer, and after chatting a few more minutes, my self-control crumbled.

“Henry . . . I can’t resist telling you . . . I have a surprise for you when you come.

“And I think I need to hang up now, or I won’t be able to resist telling you what the surprise is.”

He laughed, and teased me, but we hung up with me promising to send him the address.

* * *

No matter how busy I was, days seemed to drag by until Henry’s visit.

That Tuesday he expected to arrive about ten a.m. I woke up early and anxious.

Marietta had spent two hours with me on Monday to decide on what I’d wear and going over many of the things I’d been learning about being feminine.

I’d given him a code for the main gate, told him where to park, and where I’d be waiting for him—on a bench on a covered patio facing the visitors’ parking area.

With each car that arrived I got my hopes up, and when I finally saw Henry getting out of the latest car, I stood up and it was all I could do not to run to him and throw my arms around him—but it was still too soon to risk bouncing my breasts too much by running.

Then I noticed I was bouncing on the balls of my feet, and forced myself to stop.

Henry had spotted me right away, and hurried toward me with a bouquet of flowers, but about halfway to me, he started slowing down.

He got slower and slower and stopped about a car's length away.

His arms went limp at his sides.

I wasn't worried that he was disappointed, though, because of the expression on his face—as if he was awestruck.

I had planned to be demure, but that was impossible. I was happier than I'd ever been, and I must've been beaming.

"M-Michelle . . ." Henry murmured.

The flowers slipped from his hand, and he didn't notice.

"Michelle . . ."

He walked forward very slowly, stopped right in front of me, and gazed into my eyes.

I couldn't restrain myself anymore, and I hugged him tight—and when I did, I had a huge shock . . .

I felt my breasts pressed against him.

Almost at the same time, I felt his arms wrap around me.

I gasped . . . and Henry gasped at the same time.

I didn't want to stop hugging, but I didn't want to be too forward, so I let go and Henry did too.

"You look wonderful," I said. And he was wearing a nice cologne, too.

"You look . . ." he began, then said, "I have no words . . ."

We just gazed at each other for a minute, until I got an idea.

I took his hand and we sat down on the nearest bench, each of us turned as much as we could to face each other.

"Okay, Henry, you just sit still and watch me do something, okay?"

He nodded slowly.

I grinned, and stood up as I'd been trained to.

Many of my extensive etiquette lessons flashed through my mind, but I didn't worry . . .

I'd practiced them so much they were second nature now, especially how to rise, sit, and walk in manners that emphasize grace, poise, and elegance.

That was all enhanced by me having lost enough weight to have a trim waist, and now a mild hourglass figure.

I swayed my hips ever so slightly as I stepped over to the flowers on the ground.

Henry blurted out an apology and I urged him to sit still to prevent him from rushing over to pick them up, and he complied.

I stopped beside the flowers, not in front or behind them from Henry's perspective.

Turning to face Henry, I smiled as I studied his astonished face, and I kept my back straight and upright and my knees together as I bent my knees to lower myself enough to pick up the flowers to my side, and then I rose, grinning the whole time.

I stepped back over to the bench and sat back down.

"This is me, now," I whispered.

"Dear God, Michelle . . . you're . . . you're . . ."

When he gave up trying to say something, I did.

"Henry . . . my surprise for you . . . is that on my third Sunday here, I became a spiritual Christian, in the Chapel, right here.

"I went to a service, and right after—because of you—I told my counselor and the chaplain that I wanted to become a spiritual Christian, not just a cultural Christian, and asked if they could tell me how to do that, and they did.

"For over an hour they explained things, and they prayed with me, and I gave my whole heart to Jesus, and he changed me, Henry . . . God changed me completely.

"I feel more alive than I ever have before, and I feel his love inside me. And they gave me a Bible, and I've been reading the

Gospel of John in it every day. I've read it a bunch of times, and started reading other parts, too."

We both leaned together and hugged and cried, for I don't know how long, and I kept thanking him over and over again for him being the first person to tell me about giving my life to God.

We chatted on and on as I took him to my suite to put my flowers in water, and he was very impressed with it. I showed him all the clothes in my walk-in closet, and the view from my living room window.

We talked about how he became a Christian, about our families, he told me a lot about the Bible, and I told him about a lot of what I'd been studying at Chrysalis.

Eventually, we went to lunch in the dining area, where we talked briefly about many things, looking for common interests.

An important one was a close miss until Henry turned it into a big plus.

I love playing Pokémon and spend a lot of my spare time doing that, and a few similar games, but he loves spending a lot of his spare time playing Call of Duty, and a few games similar to that one.

It appeared we'd never enjoy playing the same game together.

But then Henry said, "How would you feel about you playing Pokémon while I play Call of Duty in the same room?

"We wouldn't be sharing a game, but we'd be close to each other. Not a shared activity, but shared presence . . ."

I thought it over, and grinned. "Kind of like an old couple sitting by the fire, the man reading a book while his wife knits. I like that a lot."

He reached across the table, took my hand, and gave it a loving squeeze, before letting go and looking shy.

After lunch we had a long hug and then went for a stroll in some of the gardens.

It was the happiest day of my life.

Then Henry lowered his voice and said, "Michelle . . . I haven't thought of Leo for one second until now, and I'm glad.

"I thought Leo was a very nice person and a good friend, but Leo wasn't masculine at all. Now I know why . . . you were hiding inside him . . . this is the real you . . . and you're the most beautiful woman I've ever seen . . ."

I was silently crying happy tears when he went on to say, "but if we want a chance . . . to consider taking our relationship further . . . I need to know about your exact anatomy . . ."

I wobbled, and he took my arm and guided me to the closest bench.

"If it's too hard to tell me now, I can wait, a while . . . if you think you'd be able to tell me soon . . . but I need to know . . ."

My tears now were from fear. I knew I had to hold nothing back, but . . . it could mean the end of any chance we had at romance. Yet, there was no escaping it, and no point in waiting.

"I have ovaries . . ." I stammered, gazing straight ahead, "but no vagina, and no uterus.

"I can't bear children. I can't have vaginal sex."

I swallowed hard before going on.

"I have a micropenis, about two inches long at most, but it never gets fully hard.

"I wear tight silicone panties to keep it flat when I'm wearing tight clothes. I have tiny testicles inside me, not on the outside, other than a small bump."

I paused again before offering what I faintly hoped might make up for some of all that . . .

"I can wear silicone panties that have a built-in prosthetic vagina . . .

"They're supposed to provide a good simulation of vaginal sex . . . and I can do all the other ways of having sex.

"I . . . I think that covers it all."

Henry nodded, looking solemn, and perhaps . . . sad.

"So . . . no natural vaginal sex and we wouldn't be able to have our own children," he finally said.

"No, we couldn't have our own children," I said as I cried.

I wanted to say we could adopt children, but that was obvious, and it couldn't fully make up for not having our own, so I didn't say it.

But I was desperate, so I did address the other issue.

"We could have sex, though.

"With a prosthesis, with my hands, and my mouth, and . . . with my anus."

I panicked as soon as I said the last phrase, and I rushed to explain as much as I could to try to help him give that idea a chance.

"I've been studying written lessons on how to do that cleanly and safely, and many men find it to be very pleasurable, and . . ."

I could tell from his expression that he didn't like the idea, and I was terrified that I shouldn't have said anything about that.

"I . . . they . . . there are . . ."

I hung my head.

"I'm sorry. I should've told you about my anatomy sooner. I.. I should've . . ."

Henry finally broke the silence with a discouraged sigh, then he said, "I'm guessing that's the hardest thing you've ever had to tell anyone."

I nodded without looking up.

"I've been studying," Henry said, "and some intersex people can bear children, and I was hoping that included you, but I knew it might not . . .

"I can't hide my disappointment, and I can't promise I can get over it, but I can tell you something important about me . . .

"You asked me on our first phone call if being part male and part female ruled you in or out for . . . us being together . . .

"Now I know we can't have normal sex and we can't have our own children . . . but that still doesn't rule us out for getting married . . ."

He was quiet, and I wasn't sure I'd heard him right.

I looked up through watery eyes.

"You've been making incredible adjustments to your life," he said, "probably far greater than I can imagine.

"I gave my life to God a long time ago, and he can help me make adjustments, too. More than anything else, I've always wanted to marry the woman God wants me to marry . . .

"So now . . . I need God to make it clear to me if he wants you and I together. I hope that won't take long, one way or the other, but I can't promise how long it will take."

We were both quiet again for a while as I cried, and we sat side by side with my head on his shoulder.

"Henry . . ." I said without moving, "if God wanted to change your heart about my missing female parts . . . would you . . . would you want me . . . ?"

I don't know why I asked.

Maybe to try to end our relationship now, maybe so I could focus on guys that already knew what to expect and already didn't mind.

But whatever caused me to ask, I didn't expect his answer.

"I want you now, Michelle.

"I love you, and I've wanted you since our first phone call a few weeks ago.

"I thought it wasn't possible because you weren't a Christian, but I wanted that and every other barrier to fall, because I admired you so much that you were willing to confide so much to me.

"It felt like you were baring your soul to me more deeply than any other girl ever known."

"W-what about Willow?" I asked. "Didn't she do that?"

"He—rats. *She* . . . she's already married, to some really rich dude, and they're very happily married.

"And besides, she wasn't—isn't . . . a Christian. And I was never attracted to him—*her*."

I was dizzy, so I kept my head on Henry's shoulder. Then a thought occurred to me.

"Henry . . . you said you were never attracted to him, before you corrected yourself."

"Right."

"Did you mean you were never attracted to him when you knew him as a male?"

"Right. And he was pretty when I saw him—*her!*—as a woman, at lunch, but I wasn't attracted to *her*."

"Henry . . . were you ever attracted to Leo?"

I felt him flinch, and I could feel him start breathing faster.

"Your face tormented me," he replied.

"I remember once when I was praying I asked God, if he was willing, to give me a wife with Leo's face."

I sat up and gazed at him. "You really did that?"

He nodded. "I did. And after you told me you're intersex, I got my hopes up—very high.

"But wait, Michelle, I don't want you to get *your* hopes up too high, now . . .

"I can sense God's Spirit in you now, which confirms what you told me about giving your life to God, but I have one giant barrier remaining . . ."

"Normal sex or our own children?" I asked.

"Having our own children," he said. "I already spent a lot of time thinking, praying, studying, and talking to a pastor about sex with an intersex woman, and I really struggled with some of the possibilities . . . but I finally concluded I can deal with anything as long as I believe God wants us to marry.

"I'm embarrassed to say I was so focused on that, I didn't realize how big of a disappointment it would be if we can't have children together.

"I think this may be something else I can't deal with unless God changes me.

'I told you that my only iron-clad rule was that I had to marry a Christian, and then I realized it had to be a woman, too.

"Well, now I realize that fathering children was part of the same foundation—I just never thought of that as an explicit requirement."

"So now . . ." I mused, "we just wait? See if . . . ?"

"See if God changes that in me? Maybe," Henry agreed, "but first I want to ask you something else.

"I've just made it very clear, I hope, that I want to marry you if God can change how I feel about children . . .

"You've indicated that you're very interested in the possibility of marrying me, but . . . if I can accept not fathering children . . . would you definitely want to marry me, or are you not sure yet?"

I couldn't speak at first, but Henry waited patiently.

"I love you with all my heart, Henry.

"I want to be your wife, if you think I can make you happy . . .

"I'll do anything for you that I'm capable of, but not being able to bear children isn't something they can fix."

Henry nodded.

"Michelle . . . I think . . . I think I can give that up. But even if I can, I think I need time for that . . . but I think . . ."

His eyes started watering.

"I love you so much . . ." he whispered.

"I admire you so much . . . I enjoy just being with you . . . I—"

He gasped and looked startled.

"I just thought of another problem . . ."

"Nooo . . ." I moaned.

Problems

Henry looked sad, and said, "This problem doesn't mean we can't get married, but it might mean a long engagement.

"My job as manager doesn't give me enough time off to be a decent husband. I come home, fall into bed, get up, and go back to work . . .

"As soon as you asked me to come and I couldn't, I started looking for another job with better hours, but so far . . . nothing.

"Even my family's helping me look."

I took his hand in mine, and he flinched as if shocked, but then he smiled.

"Henry, I'll wait for you forever as long as there's still a chance . . .

"Besides, until recently, I wasn't sure I could marry anyone. Now I know I want to marry you, and you alone."

Henry smiled, then furrowed his brow. "What happened to change that?"

"Well . . . I'm sure I never mentioned it to you, but did Willow ever mention that Manhattan Talent works with the Aurum Dating Service?"

He shook his head. "No, I didn't know that. Oh . . . I wonder if that might have been the private service she mentioned."

"Probably," I said. "They have wealthy men, some of whom are interested in finding an intersex wife . . .

"Wow—that's the first time I've told anyone, and it sounds crazy saying it out loud.

"I can explain it all to you later, but, these guys . . . some of them want anal sex, and I put in my profile that I won't do that."

I sighed. "I understand the theory. I believe now that it's moral for married couples to do that. I've studied the methods. I've even passed a written test. But I just didn't think I could actually do that.

"Now . . . I realize I love you so much I don't care about anything else.

"I'll do anything for you . . . I want to do anything and everything you want me to do, no matter what.

"So . . . with you . . . I know I can do that if you'd like that—or if you just want to try it.

"And if you don't want to do that, that's fine, too!" I added hastily. "I just want to be with you and satisfy you."

Henry was studying me. "What about your satisfaction, Michelle? Will it be possible for me to make you feel good? To satisfy you?"

I felt my face burning.

Slowly, I nodded.

"If you want to," I barely said. "I'd like that very much."

"How . . . how can I do that? No, scratch that.

"There's nothing I won't do to make you feel good, and you can teach me what you like after we get married."

"We'd have to experiment," I said quietly. "I don't know what might or might not work for me."

We were both quiet again, and I was thinking he was talking like our marriage was more likely than not, and that made me feel very strange.

A new, unfamiliar flavor of hope.

We got up and started strolling . . . but this time, Henry took my arm and hooked it in his. That had our sides touching while we walked, which made us walk very slowly.

"What was it you said first about anal sex today?" Henry asked. "About how it could be done?"

"Morally, cleanly, safely, and pleasurably, with pleasure for both the man and woman.

"What my lessons said is that the morality is the same as with all other forms of sex—only between a husband and wife, and only when both consent . . .

"It takes more time and effort to prep and clean up than vaginal sex, but without going into details right now, some husbands and wives who have a choice actually choose that sometimes."

"Huh," Henry grunted. "I wonder why? That surprises me."

"Guys like the feeling of tightness," I commented, parroting my lessons. "Girls like the feeling of fullness. Among other things. And many couples enjoy some variety in how they have sex sometimes."

"Huh."

"Marietta—she's my Chrysalis counselor—told me she could grant you access to some of the online lessons they have for men interested in dating or marrying intersex women. If you'd like that."

"That'd be great, Michelle," Henry replied. "I'd like that very much!"

We continued to walk and the topic turned to Henry's job search and job history, and I learned that after he graduated from college his first job had been as a stockbroker.

He quickly learned that the fastest common way to make big money as a stockbroker was to have rich friends—which Henry didn't—or cut ethical corners—which Henry refused, and his refusal seriously displeased his boss.

He'd tried to hold out until he could land any of several kinds of analyst jobs, but the stress was too much, so he took the first job he could find somewhere else . . . at the call center where I later came to work.

It was discouraging that he'd been earnestly job hunting ever since I first asked him to visit me, but so far, to no avail.

And I didn't say it, but I really disliked the idea of being married but hardly ever being able to spend time with my husband.

Henry started asking me more about all the things I'd been learning, which I enjoyed telling him about, and he was thrilled about my successful auditions and the possibility of a small movie role next year.

I also told him I was about to start swimming lessons to replace a different course I'd finished.

I asked if he knew how to swim and he said he did, so I asked him to bring his swimsuit the next time he came to visit.

I thought it would be fun, but mostly I wanted him to see me in a swimsuit.

We were out strolling again when I froze a second, and Henry noticed.

"You okay?" he asked.

I stopped completely, and almost let my shoulders slump. I shook my head.

"I need to sit down for this.

"Now *I* have another problem for us."

We headed toward an isolated bench, and I began, "I've told you about how much I've been enjoying my modeling and acting classes and rehearsals, and that I have an offer for a small role in a movie next year . . ."

"Yes . . ."

"Well, Marietta thinks there's a chance I could become famous . . ."

"Hmm . . ." Henry murmured.

When I didn't go on right away, he said, "I can easily see that.

"And you're wondering if I'd be okay with you being famous? That's something I never thought about before . . ."

"Not just that," I said. "If I become famous, then the more famous I become, the more likely people are to dig into my past."

"Oh . . . That's interesting . . ."

I stayed silent as we got to a bench and sat down, letting him ponder.

"You're right," he said a minute later. "That might be a problem."

I sighed.

"Yeah. Nobody wants to be known as the husband of an intersex woman, I guess. So I already figured that out . . .

"I won't take the one job offer I've already gotten, and I'll quit pursuing that completely."

"What?! No!

"Michelle, if we get married, *I* don't care who knows you're intersex.

"I assumed you wouldn't want anyone to know, but that was a foolish assumption on my part. If you don't mind people finding out about that, I certainly don't."

I stared at him in amazement.

"Are you serious? You wouldn't mind that?"

"No, not a bit. I'd rather they not know about the specific symptoms of your intersexuality, but I think that's kind of like any guy wouldn't want anyone else to see his wife naked."

"Wow . . . okay, I—wait . . . then why did you say it might be a problem?"

"Oh, not other people knowing you're intersex . . . what might bother me is you being famous."

I couldn't help but laugh. "That bothers you more than intersex?"

"Yeah . . ." he said with a half-smile. "My first thought was that I wouldn't care if you're famous, but I immediately reconsidered it.

"I think that might actually challenge me, Michelle . . . seriously . . . because I'm not famous.

"I didn't think I was that shallow, but I guess I am, because I think that would really bother me, although I don't know why."

Dang. We keep having problems and we aren't even married yet. Then I thought of something.

"Henry, my psychologist has been talking to me some about how to handle success.

"I never imagined that might be a problem, but I've been surprised at how big an issue that can be, and I just remembered a comment he made about how fame is often equated with success. He—"

"That's it!" Henry exclaimed.

"*That's* what was in the back of my mind . . . ! If you're famous, and I'm not, will I feel like you're successful and I'm not . . . ?"

I wanted to say something to reassure him somehow, but I couldn't think of anything right away, so we just sat there, both of us thinking.

Then I saw him relax, then smile.

"I can deal with that, Michelle.

"Now that I know what was bothering me, and know it's just a stereotype about men being successful while their wives are in the background, that won't bother me at all.

"My success is rooted in God's love for me, not what happens in life."

He laughed, then added, "Which is good, because if word gets out that you're intersex, that might increase your fame."

I stared at him as he gazed at me.

"You . . . you changed your mind, and your attitude . . . just like that? That fast?"

"Well . . . yeah . . . once you gave me the clue as to what it was that was bothering me."

I thought of all the many sessions I'd had with Dr. Crowley, and how painful some of them were, and how hard some of my changes had been.

Then I thought Henry's mental stability based on his faith in God might make him a perfect husband for me.

*

We went on to other, more enjoyable topics, but eventually, reluctantly, Henry needed to head home.

The first time we decided it was time for him to go, we found other things to talk about instead.

The second and third times, too.

When we finally got to his car, I cried and we hugged, and this time we didn't stop hugging for a long time.

I wanted him to kiss me, but he didn't.

I'd never wanted anyone to kiss me before, and I never knew how powerful that desire could be.

Halfway home, Henry pulled off the highway and called me.

"Michelle . . ." he began after our hellos, "my attitude about having children of my own is going to change.

"I know it. I don't know how I can know since it hasn't happened yet, but I'm certain. God's changing me.

"I love you, and I want to spend the rest of my life with you, and I'm going to come back as soon as I get a good job and ask you to marry me."

I struggled to talk through my crying.

"Henry . . . today I talked to you about the hardest things I'll ever have to talk about . . . and I didn't scare you away.

"I love you more than ever. I'll be praying for you to find a good job, and do you mind if I ask some of my friends here to pray with me about that?"

Of course, he didn't mind, and he brought up the possibility of us adopting children.

I told him I liked that idea, but my psychologist thinks I should wait a few years to get used to my new life before adding children, and Henry thought that sounded wise.

Although neither of us wanted to hang up, we finally did, and I bawled like a baby as I lay on my bed and cried out to God with thankfulness and asking him to help Henry get a job he liked.

Preferably one that made use of his business degree, since I knew he'd like that.

Aurum Date

As soon as I finished praying, I called Marietta, and I hardly said much before she figured most of it out.

She was thrilled for me, and said she and Charles would start praying for both of us and for a better job for Henry.

The next morning, she came over early and ate breakfast with me.

"Michelle," Marietta said, "I think it's fair to call Henry's visit a date, wouldn't you?"

"Yes," I agreed. "The best date ever, and a pending marriage proposal from the most wonderful man in the world!"

"Yes, but it's the first date you've ever had, including before you came to Chrysalis, right?"

"Yes . . ."

"And everything you've told me about your date yesterday sounds exciting, with all its highlights and disappointments . . . but you have nothing to compare it to."

She let me consider that a moment before she went on.

"I know you're excited about marrying Henry, but I have an idea that I'd like you to consider and discuss with Dr. Crowley.

"Since you grew up in less than ideal conditions, you know now some of the ways that created risks for your ability to form lasting relationships."

"Yes," I agreed again. "But I love Henry and only Henry, so it's either him or no one for me.

I'm sorry if that's bad for Aurum or Chrysalis or Manha—"

"No, no," Marietta interrupted. "Don't even think that, Michelle.

"I accept your decision that you have no interest in possible romance through our dating service, and no one here will mind that at all.

"We'll all be very happy for you and Henry."

"Okay . . . then what do you want me to talk to Doc about?"

"You know the difference between a casual date and a romantic date now, right?"

"Absolutely, yes," I replied.

"And our dating service is for romantic dates, right?"

"Yes . . . that's all I've ever heard."

"It is. But I'm suggesting an exception—a casual date—with no romantic intentions—just so you'll have at least one experience to compare Henry to."

She held up a hand to stop me from objecting.

"Please let me finish.

"You and this date would both know beforehand that it's not romantic, and the man will know you're planning to marry someone else.

"It might benefit you simply to know first-hand what a casual date with someone else is like.

"And it might benefit him by giving him some non-romantic social experience with a beautiful woman.

"And . . . I'm not urging you to do this, I'm only urging you to talk to Dr. Crowley about it.

"If he thinks there would be no value or it might be counterproductive, then it's out. That's fine. But if he thinks it might be a good idea, then I think you should consider it."

I shook my head firmly. "No, I'm sorry, Marietta, but I won't date someone else behind Henry's back."

Marietta smiled. "Well, I agree with that.

"If this casual date is a good idea, then I think you should definitely tell Henry about it.

"In fact, maybe he should get a veto. If the doctor thinks it might be worthwhile to you."

I thought it over a long time while she waited patiently, and my mind ran through some of the many problems I'd learned I might have from not having a father and my mom being . . . less than an ideal mother.

Buried effects from guilt, fear, occasional abandonment, shame, and dozens of other things . . . and the most dangerous of all: potential difficulty in maintaining a stable marriage relationship.

It also occurred to me that I hadn't told Henry about all that yet, and I should. Soon.

I sighed heavily.

I loved Henry and I wanted us to be happily married forever . . . which meant I should do whatever I can to try to ensure that my past doesn't come back to ruin my relationship with him.

"Will you come explain your idea to Doc?" I asked.

"Of course. And if he dismisses the idea, I'll apologize for even thinking it."

"But if he does think it's a good idea, I'm not really interested in any of the guys I got letters from."

Marietta nodded. "I have one guy in mind.

"He's dated here before, and the girls told me how the dates went.

"If—and only if—Dr. Crowley thinks this is a good idea, I think this guy might be suitable, and if you give me permission, I could try to set up a date for you—just here on campus.

"Just walking the grounds and sharing a meal. And talking."

"And no touching? None at all?"

"Zero touching.

"And I think we could trust this guy to keep his word on that. If you'd like, I could keep you both in sight the whole time so I could intervene if you wave at me."

We were quiet again a few moments, then I asked, "Who?"

"Roger. He's the one whose letter you liked the best."

"Why didn't things work out with his other dates?" I asked.

"You've seen his photo now," she replied. "He's a good bit older than you and most of Aurum's other members.

"Some felt his looks in person were worse than in his photo. He's divorced, overweight, and . . . his social skills are awkward."

"Dang . . . now I feel sorry for him."

"Feeling sorry for him would be a terrible reason to have a romantic date with him.

"But he's a Christian, and the other two girls did say he was kind, considerate, and extremely intelligent."

We met with Dr. Crowley that afternoon, and Marietta told him about the idea, and Doc asked me what I liked and disliked about it.

He ended up thinking it was a good idea, mostly because of my lack of a father figure while growing up and my very meager socialization before coming to Chrysalis.

The decision was up to me, and after a while I said, "I know neither of you would suggest this if you didn't think this is in my best interest . . ."

They both nodded.

"Okay, then. I very much don't like the idea, but I'll do it just based on your recommendation, if Henry says it's okay, and after I review some lessons on casual dating.

"But I also have another reason . . . there've been things about Chrysalis I haven't liked from the very beginning that turned out to be great.

"I can't help but wonder if maybe this could be another thing like that."

Then we prayed together, I went back to my regular routine, and I texted Henry and asked him to call me when he could.

* * *

It was very late when Henry called, having just gotten home, and he sounded very tired but happy to be talking to me.

Until I told him what I needed to talk about.

He hated the idea.

He raised lots of objections and ranted a bit against Marietta and Doc, and questioned their motivations.

That's what reminded me I needed to tell him about all the psychological problems I might have buried inside from a neglected and unstable childhood—some of which Doc had already helped me dredge up and start healing from.

So, when I mentioned that, Henry wanted me to tell him all about it, despite how tired he was.

I told him about it for five or ten minutes, which barely scratched the surface, but then I insisted on stopping so Henry could get to bed.

We agreed I'd tell him everything over future phone calls, but Henry quietly told me to go ahead and take Doc's advice—on the condition I call or text Henry right after the date and tell him everything was still okay between us.

* * *

Marietta set it up and Roger came to Chrysalis planning to spend two hours with me, but we stretched it to four, and we became good friends—but only friends.

He turned out to be a wonderful man—definitely kind and considerate—and I thought he was handsome in a rugged, rough way.

And I didn't think he weighed too much. I could see why other women might not find him physically attractive, but I did.

I learned a fair amount about him and his interests, and he was full of questions about me, exploring my interests, past, present, and future.

There was nothing he wasn't curious about.

As soon as our date was over, I thought I knew what his most likely problem with romance was, and why I never could have been suitable as his wife.

And I told Marietta, so she could pass it on to his dating coach . . .

Roger, in my opinion, needed someone who was his intellectual equal, or close to it.

And I knew that Marietta and Doc had been right to encourage me to go on this date so I'd have something to compare my relationship with Henry to.

Now I had even more confidence that Henry was perfect for me, and I could look back on this whenever Henry and I got into arguments.

I texted Henry while I knew he was at work, so I kept it short.

"Date's over.

"Nice guy. I don't love him.

"I love you.

"I want to marry you as soon as we can afford enough time together.

"Because I'm never going to want you to stop hugging me."

It took a while, but Henry texted back. "When I propose, do you want me to have a ring then, or would you rather pick one out after the proposal?"

I couldn't study for a long time after that reply.

I was way too happy.

I wasn't formally engaged to Henry, but informally, we were completely committed to each other.

With Henry wanting me even with my biological and psychological shortcomings, I wanted to give him every reason I could to never regret it.

"A piece of string to tie around my finger," I texted back. "So we can choose my ring together."

Grand Audition

Henry and I were extremely happy even though we were frustrated.

To avoid tiring him too much, we decided to limit our communication to two texts each way after he got home each night except on Tuesdays.

Tuesdays were his days for job interviews—in-person if they were in or near NYC, or online if they were anywhere else.

He had two interviews on two Tuesdays in a row, and two seemed promising, but one ultimately turned him down and the other was still pending.

The rest of his Tuesdays were for job hunting and for us to talk and pray on the phone three times—once in the morning, once midday, and once in the evening.

We were patiently optimistic.

A month after he came to see me, on the third Tuesday, I ignored an incoming text from Marietta while Henry and I were having our morning talk, which we had to end so he could start an online interview.

After we hung up, I checked the text.

"Call me. Urgent."

Huh. As long as I'd been at Chrysalis, nothing had ever been urgent. Schedules, yes, but as long as you weren't late, that didn't count as urgent.

"I've cancelled all your training for today," Marietta said without a hello, "and your session with Dr. Crowley.

"We're going to the City, and you need to get ready. Wear your little black dress.

"You want to look as good as possible, and as soon as you're dressed, go to the salon. Jennifer will be waiting to fix your hair."

"Uh, okay. What's up?"

"You have an audition.

"It's for sort of a fashion gig, but Mrs. Forth kind of insisted.

"*Please* tell me you don't mind."

"Oh, no, I don't mind at all. I—"

"Oh, good!" Marietta said, followed by a fast sigh. "I'll pick you up at the salon."

*

Marietta's face was flushed when she got to the salon a few minutes before Jennifer was done with me.

Once we were on the highway, she was still a bit out of breath and trying to force herself to calm down.

"Hey, listen," she said rapidly, "you told me you're okay with the public finding out about you being intersex, and I passed that along to Mrs. Forth.

"And she told me this morning that she told the CEO of the company you're going to audition with today. Kind of like you telling a date, before you date him.

"She thought this company needed to know before they decide to hire you, to make sure it wouldn't be a deal-breaker before things got too far along . . ."

She took a deep breath and blew it out.

I giggled. "I'd think maybe I should be nervous, but I think you're nervous enough for both of us."

Marietta laughed, and that helped her relax.

"Okay, Michelle . . . is Henry still off on Tuesdays?"

"Yes. From his full-time job, that is. He works hard at job hunting and doing interviews on his day off."

"Think he could skip that today to be at your audition?"
"What?! Really?! Let me call him!"

I called, and Henry had long since finished his video interview, so he answered right away.
I explained what was going on, and he was extremely excited.

"Tell him to wear his nicest suit," Marietta told me, and I passed it along.
I also gave Henry the address and what time to meet us in the lobby, based on the car's GPS estimate of our arrival time.

Traffic was very heavy, but Marietta's Tesla made the ride very relaxed, and she was able to calm down completely as we talked about possible wedding plans for once Henry had a better job.
Then I ruined her newly calm attitude when I asked her to be my matron of honor, and it was a good thing the car was driving itself, because she started crying pretty hard.

She said we'd be welcome to get married at the Chrysalis chapel and honeymoon in my suite if we wanted to, and that sounded perfect to me, if Henry liked it.

When we were a few blocks from Manhattan Talent, Marietta walked me through using her phone to open a valet app and tap a button on it.
When we pulled up in front, she put the car in valet-mode as two men appeared to open our doors for us.
Then they held open the front doors to the lobby, and I ran into Henry's arms.

Marietta only gave us a few seconds before herding us on. "C'mon, guys, they're holding the elevator for us."

It wasn't other riders holding the elevator for us, it was someone in a uniform holding it just for us. He got in too, and used a card to take the elevator straight to Manhattan Talent.

It felt like we were being treated like we owned the place.

At least Henry and I got to hug in the elevator, because once it opened again, it was bedlam.

People standing right outside the elevator immediately whisked us off to a private area where several other people were waiting for us.

Some introductions were made, but they were too fast to remember.

Most of them stood back when one man approached and looked me over, and then Henry.

"The black satin gown for Miss Loren, Louboutin heels, and diamonds."

"Full set?" someone asked.

The man looked insulted.

"Yes, sir, full set."

"Peak Lapel Tuxedo for the gentleman," the man barked. "Classic black."

At that, people started pulling me one way, and Henry another.

My objections and questions were ignored, but I saw Marietta following behind my little crowd.

"Marietta, do they think Henry's here to audition? Can you straighten them out?"

"They're going to fix him up to be your official escort," she called out.

After I was dragged into a changing room, flying hands took my clothes off—all except my silicone panties, thank God.

Just as quickly, I was dressed again and put into a makeup chair, and all my carefully crafted makeup was stripped off and new makeup was applied.

Then a hair stylist refixed my hair to her own satisfaction.

Two security guards brought the diamonds, and I had to sign for them.

Then more hands arrayed me with dangle earrings, a necklace with pendant, a small brooch, a bracelet on my left wrist, and a ring on my right hand.

Other than the diamonds, I'd been through all that before multiple times, but never in such a hurry.

After the first couple of minutes, I just started relaxing and enjoying it, almost like it was entertainment, just for me.

Marietta was nearby looking amused, and I smiled while wondering what this experience was like for Henry.

* * *

As the hair stylist was finishing with me, a small group of people came in, including Mrs. Forth . . . and then . . . Henry.

I stood, eyes locked on the love of my life, who looked stunning to me and stunned as he gazed at me.

As far as I was concerned at that moment, he was the only other person in the room.

We approached each other slowly and melted into each other's arms, and I cried, hard.

Then . . . my Henry kissed me.

Dear God, he kissed me.

Then he broke our hug to step back and hold up one of his hands.

I couldn't focus through my tears at first, but something was dangling from it.

A piece of yarn.

Henry got down on one knee and asked me to marry him.

I managed to say yes, and he tied that string on my finger, and then we hugged again.

I don't know how long we were like that, but eventually we were pulled apart, and people started fussing over Henry's jacket as they worked me over with makeup again.

Minutes later, when I was calm enough to listen, Henry stood beside me while Mrs. Forth sat on a stool in front of us.

"That was quite a surprise, Michelle, and we're all very happy for you, but we have some very important business to take care of.

"Can you do it?"

That sobered me right up, and I straightened up my posture.

"Yes, ma'am, I can."

"Good. This isn't so much an audition as a reception and negotiation.

"There's a brand new cosmetics company about to launch internationally, but it will be based here in Manhattan.

"They're now at the stage to select their brand spokesmodel, and after watching videos of you modeling and acting and talking to your instructors, they've chosen you.

"If we can all agree on the terms.

"The name of the company is Splendeur—which is French for magnificence or grandeur in addition to splendor—and that's their makeup you're wearing now.

"The name will be pronounced in a variety of ways, but the company founder is French, and *you* will always use the French pronunciation, splahn-DUR."

I pronounced it several times, and she seemed satisfied that I wasn't mangling it, and she continued.

"They're here—waiting—to meet you in person.

"This young man of yours, I'm told," she said with barely a nod in his direction, "has a business degree and is looking for a career change.

"If we can conclude a contract with Splendeur, you're going to need a professional manager.

"Henry, is it?

"Henry can be your manager, and we have an expert—Chip Calvert—who can mentor him, starting a few minutes ago.

"This is a lot to take in and cope with," she concluded.

"Can you do it?"

I paused, then stood up, and spoke with composure.

"I can, Mrs. Forth, on two conditions.

"First, I have to hug you, to thank you for that first day we met.

"And I'm going to cry again when I do that.

"Then, I want to discuss this makeup with the two makeup artists who put it on me, then fixed it, and are about to need to fix it again.

"Then I'll be ready."

We did that, and Mrs. Forth had a few tears, too.

Then . . . it was showtime.

Splendeur

For the next few hours, I combined my acting and modeling skills during a reception-like event, including a catered buffet table which I ignored.

I acted as I thought appropriate for the Splendeur brand ambassador—which was easy—and I put my engagement out of my mind and treated Henry as my manager—which was very hard.

I met Splendeur's CEO—Madam Giselle Dufresne—and several others of their executives and board members, and without the introductions being rushed, I did a good job of remembering their names and titles.

Then I tried to be as gracious as I'd been taught as I "worked the room," making warm small talk and using their names to help them feel welcome at Manhattan Talent's headquarters.

There were two photographers taking candids, one from each company, and there was a photo op for a while where each of the guests—one or two at a time—got to have a formal photo with me in front of a Manhattan Talent backdrop.

As I'd been trained, I made sure there was a moment with each guest where we were gazing at the camera and smiling, but as often as possible when they stepped up, I smiled as we gazed at each other and shook hands—kissing cheeks if they initiated it, and the photographers took shots then, too.

And for the camera-facing shot, I took my cues from the guests—if they reached to put their arm around my waist, I let them and I put my arm around theirs, otherwise, I kept my arms by my side.

Halfway through, they started congratulating me on my engagement, showcasing our industry's famous lightning-speed gossip.

I also got to meet Raven Montague, the founder of Manhattan Talent, Chrysalis, and Aurum, and she was as beautiful as she was gracious.

Henry and Chip stood near one of the doors most of the time, which allowed me to work my way past him repeatedly so we could at least smile and say hello to each other once in a while.

On one pass, Henry whispered to me that he'd overheard someone in a group near him say, "Can you imagine what it would've been like to have met Audrey Hepburn at the beginning of her career?" and another replied, "We don't have to imagine."

That was hard to believe, and to understand.

I was just me.

The crowd size kept growing, and many people introduced themselves to me, but it quickly became too many to remember.

After about an hour of mixing with jazz playing in the background, Mrs. Forth took to a small stage, brought me up to introduce me, then made a short speech touting Splendeur, pointed out some of Splendeur's leaders, and toasting them.

After that, most of the crowd started fading away, until it was mostly just the business decision-makers on both sides, plus me, Henry, Marietta, and Chip. Then someone decided it was time for us to go to the board room to try to finalize the deal.

The board room had a long table, naturally, with fancy chairs all around, but also another row of plain seats along the side walls.

The table was for the big shots and the outer seats were for support staff.

Mrs. Forth was seated at one end, Madam Dufresne at the other end, and I was seated in the middle of the side closest to the windows.

Henry was on my left, and a board member of Splendeur named Walton Strakes was on my right. Marietta was seated behind me.

There was a bit of what seemed to me like tug of war between Mrs. Forth and Madam Dufresne, as to who would make a proposal first, each wanting the other to start. Madam Dufresne apparently lost.

After a little fanfare, she announced with her beautiful French accent, "We want Miss Loren to represent Splendeur exclusively . . . she won't work for anyone else in cosmetics, obviously, and any fashion or acting jobs have to be approved by us in advance.

"She must live in Midtown Manhattan so she's always available on short notice for dinners and other events.

"Our terms are renewable indefinitely, but cancelable at any time if she in any way brings disrepute to the brand.

"For this service, we'd like to propose a very generous offer of a quarter-million per year, a hundred thousand signing bonus, and of course, all business-related travel and event expenses for Miss Loren."

To me, that sounded like they opened the door to Fort Knox, but I think I kept a straight face on the outside.

Mrs. Forth looked and sounded insulted.

"Most of your service request is fine, subject to two exceptions and a lot of fine-tuning, but the compensation isn't even close to acceptable. Let me tell you why.

"Your firm's first spokesmodel is the single most important part of capturing international public interest for a brand new company.

"You need the very best possible, and they must be truly extraordinary. Michelle Loren is a once-in-a-century opportunity, not only for you, but for us . . .

"We're certainly not going to let her go for a song, and if you can't afford or aren't willing to pay what she's worth, there are others who will. Perhaps one of your major competitors."

Madam Dufresne calmly asked for a counter-proposal.

"Five million a year to start," Mrs. Forth said, "increasing twenty-five percent per year, a million dollar signing bonus, up to twelve hundred hours per year, all business-related travel and event expenses for Miss Loren *and* her manager, and a stipulation that her manager may keep her in his physical sight at all times."

Five . . . million . . . dollars . . . ?! A year?!

I kept my outward composure, but I think that deserved an Academy Award. That was insane money for a twenty-two year old fashion novice.

"That would make her one of the highest paid spokesmodels in history," Madam Dufresne objected with an edge to her voice.

"That might be appropriate for an A-list celebrity, but Miss Loren is a complete unknown!"

Mrs. Forth countered, "And that's one of the reasons she's so extraordinarily valuable to you.

"She has no public past to tarnish your brand and no social media, ever.

"Your PR people can create her social media and interact with her fans for her, which could more than double your positive exposure.

"You can choose when to release her biographical information, doubling positive exposure again.

"Miss Loren is also very young, which gives Splendeur at least an extra decade with an iconic face over anyone else half as suitable.

"You can choose from thousands of other models for a meager hourly rate, but Splendeur's market cap won't break a hundred million.

"There's only one Michelle Loren, and with her, Splendeur is a billion-dollar company."

The two titans bickered back and forth a few minutes, while I tried not to faint.

Then my acting training kicked in, and I regained my composure by pretending I was acting this scene in a movie.

When the two women seemed close to losing their tempers with each other, I raised my hand.

It worked.

They paused long enough to look at me, and I rose to my feet and turned a bit toward the Splendeur end of the table.

"Madam Dufresne, may I say that I've had your new products applied three times today, I've spoken to our makeup artists who applied it, they've studied your promotional material . . .

"And we're all very highly pleased with the exceptional quality and conscientious ingredients . . .

"I would be proud to represent Splendeur, and I hope we can meet in the middle so I may have that great honor."

Then I sat down, as gracefully as I knew how, and gave a demure glance around the room, just as Marietta had drilled into me during etiquette classes.

It seemed to me the feeling in the room shifted and Mr. Strakes spoke next.

"Giselle," he began, looking at Madam Dufresne, "I'll support an offer right in the middle."

She gave a barely perceptible nod, and he turned toward Mrs. Forth, who looked completely calm again.

"Would that be acceptable to Manhattan Talent?" he asked.

Mrs. Forth replied, "Two and a half million a year to start, increasing twelve and a half percent per year, and a half-million-dollar signing bonus . . .

"But keeping a twelve-hundred hour annual cap and all business-related travel and event expenses for Miss Loren and her manager, and his constant oversight provision.

"On the service side, we may propose outside contracts in fashion only—non-cosmetics-related—and in acting.

"Splendeur may veto up to half the fashion gigs and a quarter of the acting gigs per year. Up to ten percent of the vetoes you don't use in one year roll over for one extra year.

"Bear in mind that as Miss Loren's fame increases, so does the power of her representation of Splendeur at no expense to Splendeur.

"We'll accept that if there are no further counter-proposals," Mrs. Forth concluded.

The Splendeur people exchanged glances, with most of them obviously deferential to Mr. Strakes, who nodded to Madam Dufresne.

"We accept," Madam Dufresne announced, and most everyone but the titans and I applauded and cheered.

I rose, as did most people pretty quickly, and I worked the room just as Marietta had taught me.

I went around and shook everyone's hands, thanked them very sincerely by name, and made frequent comments to the Splendeur team about how much I was looking forward to working with them—which was completely true.

After I made a full circuit around the room, most of the Manhattan Talent people started leaving.

The lawyers on both teams went to another room to do whatever they do, and one of our public relations people went into a corner with a Splendeur public relations person.

Two Manhattan Talent liaisons to the Splendeur team kept me the center of attention with the Splendeur leaders, and nearby, Henry, Marietta, and Chip Calvert kept me company.

All the Splendeur folks wanted me to come to dinner parties at their homes, and Chip informed them that Henry would be managing my schedule and he would start coordinating with a Splendeur liaison as soon as they appointed one.

Eventually, Marietta was able to extract me, Henry, and Chip, followed by the two diamond guards, and said she was taking us to a private lounge area for us to recover and start discussing some important issues.

When we got there, though, she ushered Henry and I through the door and closed it behind us, saying, "Take a few minutes, and open the door when you're ready for us."

Happily Ever After

Henry pulled me into his arms and started kissing me before the door clicked shut.

I started getting hot from the kissing, his hands caressing my back, the pressure of my breasts against his chest, and feeling his bulge pressing into me.

I tried to pull away before it became too much, but Henry didn't let me . . . and moments later I started trembling and went limp.

He was alarmed, and he held me up as he moved me to a sofa.

"Michelle, are you alright?! Are you having a seizure? Should I get help?"

"N-no . . ." I panted. "That was . . . excitement . . ."

"Excitement? What—wait . . . you mean you just . . ."

I nodded. "I think so . . . based on . . . what I've read . . . a climax is . . . supposed to feel like."

"Just from that?!" he exclaimed.

I nodded again, and he dropped onto the sofa beside me. I climbed into his lap and we wrapped our arms around each other.

"D-dr. Crowley . . . my psychologist . . . says there's something called . . . um . . . psychogenic . . . orgasm . . . triggered by, uh . . . emotion or non-sexual . . . physical contact . . ."

Concerned this might disappoint Henry, I was trying to think of what to say next when he laughed.

"There's just one surprise after another with you.

"Is it safe to kiss you again?"

I answered with a kiss.

Then I whispered, "You interrupted a multimillion dollar business deal to ask me to marry you . . .

"That was pretty surprising."

Henry cooed, "I vowed to myself that I was going to ask you the next time I saw you in person.

"I would've asked you in the lobby downstairs if we hadn't been rushed up here, and then we were yanked apart.

"Once I got to you again, I wasn't going to let anything stop me."

We hugged and kissed and caressed a little more, and I shed a few tears from happiness, until we felt guilty at making Marietta and Chip wait.

*

Henry opened the door, and Marietta and Chip came in with a tray of drinks while the diamond guards came in and took the jewelry.

"Oh, Henry," I commented, "around here if a glass has a black band around the base or stem, it's non-alcoholic."

"Right, Chip already told me, and that's all I've had so I can stay as sharp as possible."

"Oh!" I cried out as an awful thought occurred to me.

"Marietta, Mrs. Forth told me I did very well, but maybe she was being polite since other people were around.

"Do you think she might actually be upset with me for interfering in the meeting?"

Marietta laughed. "No, not a chance. I worked for her for a few months, and she always says exactly what she thinks."

She laughed again.

"And she always starts with an offer that's twice what she's willing to settle for. You just got us there faster while avoiding anyone building up grudges.

"And your speech gave them one more example of why you're so much better than someone who's just a good model.

"Everything you did from beginning to end demonstrated that."

Then Marietta toasted our engagement, and as we sat down, she said, "Everyone's excited for you both, of course, but . . . Splendeur doesn't want you to change your last name . . . and that's very important to them . . ."

Henry and I gazed at each other, and he said, "I love your name like it is, too, and I won't feel slighted at all if you keep it.

"In fact . . . that would reinforce my feeling that I'm marrying royalty."

"Henry!" I exclaimed. "What do you mean? You know my past . . . I'm a nobody!"

He took my hands in his.

"Michelle, you've never been a nobody.

"Never.

"You just didn't know until recently just how extraordinary you are, in countless ways.

"Mrs. Forth knows. Everyone here knows . . ."

"Everyone," Marietta said tenderly.

I hugged Henry and burst into tears, sobbing without caring who was around.

*

After a few minutes, my crying quieted down and I slipped off my shoes, curled my legs up under me, and snuggled up close to Henry.

"Feel up to listening?" Henry asked.

I nodded.

"While they were fitting me into this tux Chip was explaining a lot—and I mean a *lot*, and fast—about what was going on, and how Mrs. Forth wanted me to be your personal manager, and I agreed.

"And I assumed you'd agree."

I nodded.

"And because you'll be my only client, there's a lot of manager things I don't need to learn about. And Chip's already started giving me a crash course in my most important responsibilities.

"The single most important thing is that I have to protect you at all your events . . . making sure you don't get any spiked drinks or food, no one touches you inappropriately, and they don't ask you to do anything out of line with your recovery from surgery—which I need to get the details on.

"Are you okay with that?"

I sobbed a couple of times, but nodded.

Then Henry frowned, and said something in a shaky voice that wasn't like him at all.

"Well . . . all of a sudden I'm not sure I'm ready for all this . . ."

His eyes pleaded with Chip and Marietta.

"Guys . . . I have a business degree from a small public college and my most recent performance review said I'm 'great with angry customers on the phone.'

"How can I be sure I won't ruin this for Michelle?"

Chip grinned, and clapped him on the shoulder. "You just did it. You weren't sure about something, and you asked us for help.

"You didn't let pride get in your way, and that's a key trait of every good manager I've ever worked with.

"And if it's okay with you, I'm planning to be your shadow for the next few weeks. And after that, you can call or text me anytime.

"I'd offer to stay close longer, but after this push, you'll be a seasoned pro. No question about it."

Henry exhaled sharply, let his shoulders relax, and gave me a sheepish smile.

"You trust me that much?" he asked.

"With my life, Henry."

"Well, then . . ." Henry went on, "I have what may be a very delicate question for you.

"I thought of this when the financial terms were agreed on . . .

"How would you feel about both of us living off only your income?"

"All I want is to spend as much time with you as I can," I whimpered. "Every day and every night."

"I feel the same way," Henry said.

"But the stereotype of the husband being the breadwinner is deeply ingrained in our society, so please be sensitive to that.

"If you tease me about that someday just in fun, that might hurt even if you don't mean it that way."

"I promise, Henry . . . I promise.

"I think that'll be easy, because I'll always think that it's *us* earning it together, not just me.

"You'll be watching over me and protecting me and managing our money so I can be carefree enough to pose and act and talk to people like I need to."

He kissed the top of my head and said, "And you just raised another issue.

"We need to decide how to formalize me being your manager and how we'll handle money. Do you want us to have separate bank accounts so that—"

"Please no, Henry!" I pleaded. "Please . . . you handle all our money. Any way you think best for us.

"*Please* don't ask me to manage money."

"Okay, okay," he laughed. "So are you okay with me quitting my tech support job once you get your signing bonus?"

I nodded eagerly.

"Marietta . . ." he asked, "how long do you think it might be before the Splendeur contract is signed? And when would Michelle actually get the signing bonus?"

Marietta smiled, then winced.

"This will be one of Manhattan Talent's standard contracts, so it can be fast, and Splendeur wants it finalized and signed today," she replied.

"Their office is only a ten minute walk from here, and Madam Dufresne and their CFO will come back as soon as the lawyers are ready.

"They should bring the check with them, but it will take Manhattan Talent a few days to send a deposit to Michelle.

"I can cover our expenses that long—or longer," Henry said.

"But . . ." Marietta continued, "They're going to expect Michelle in photo and video shoots starting tomorrow.

"And in between those they'll want you both at luncheons and dinner parties every night leading up to their big public announcement, probably on a Friday evening two or three weeks from now.

"They've already been teasing it for weeks, but were having trouble finding their face.

'They found out about Michelle on Friday, and realized she'd be the spokesmodel of their dreams.

"I didn't find out until this morning.

"The public announcement will be a very big deal, probably at the Waldorf Astoria's Grand Ballroom, with a thousand or more people . . .

"Insiders from big media, social media, beauty, fashion, socialites, investors, brand partners, and more.

"It'll be the official launch of the product line, but the star of the show won't be cases full of makeup, it'll be Michelle Loren wearing Splendeur makeup and making everyone who sees her want to be just like her."

I sat up some and pulled away from Henry enough to look him in the eyes.

"What's wrong, Henry? I felt your muscles tense up and you haven't relaxed them."

He sighed. "It sounds like I need to quit my job *today*—with no notice, and I've always considered that a bad lack of professional courtesy."

Chip asked, "Would you quit in a heartbeat if Michelle was in a car accident and needed you to stay with her in the hospital?"

"Of course I would," Henry replied. "I'd use vacation if I had any, but I'd be by her side no matter what."

"Well," Chip said, "the only difference is that Michelle needs you by her side for something wonderful instead of something tragic."

Everyone was quiet a few moments, waiting on Henry.

"Chip," he finally said, "you and I are going to be good friends.

"Oh, and Michelle, I can cover the cost of you staying in a hotel here until their check clears, so you won't have to go back and forth from the Hamptons."

"We can help with a hotel," Marietta said. "We have contracted discounts at several hotels within a few blocks, and we also have a good relationship with an apartment hunting service.

"You may not have much time for apartment hunting, so having someone filter out the unsuitable units can save a lot of time . . .

"And Michelle, I can have someone bring your wardrobe. And Henry, you can borrow that tux until you get your attire sorted, but you'll have to sign for it. And if it's pinned, we'll get them to stitch it real quick."

Then I yelped and clapped my hand over my mouth, and Marietta was the first to ask me what was wrong.

"When will we have time for a wedding?" I moaned. "And a honeymoon?

"I'm so tired of waiting . . ."

Then Marietta's eyebrows went up. "Could you wait . . . another month or so? If it takes that long to have enough time off for a decent honeymoon?"

I exchanged glances with Henry.

"I suppose so," I sighed. "If we have to."

Henry snapped his fingers with a gleam in his eye and a quick glance at Marietta before gazing at me.

"If we're waiting that long to get married anyway . . . if it's okay with you, Michelle, picture this . . .

"Splendeur rolls out their new brand, their new product line, and their new spokesmodel in two weeks, with millions in paid advertising and millions more in free news headlines.

"Then . . . two weeks after that . . . their new superstar gets married, and Splendeur throws a huge reception for us with the same media and insiders in attendance!"

"That's what I was thinking," Marietta said with a huge grin.

"And we'll have leading designers fighting over who gets to give you a free rush-job wedding gown."

I guess I didn't look enthusiastic enough, so Henry said, "Michelle, we can get married as soon as you want, but you're going to have long work days and short nights for several weeks, at least."

I took a deep breath and let it out slowly as they all studied me.

"I'd rather get married tomorrow and honeymoon for a week or two and then start everything with Splendeur. But . . . under the circumstances . . .

"I agree. Your plan's probably the best way for us to do this."

Satisfied, the three of them kept chatting quickly and excitedly, and I only half paid attention as I started practicing the relaxation exercises my acting coach taught me.

Henry was going to work on getting a copy of my birth certificate so I could get a passport . . .

Marietta was texting someone to bring a new phone to Henry for him to use for business only . . .

Henry agreed for us that we'd have a second, low-key reception after the honeymoon—at Chrysalis, for all the wonderful staff.

Chip talked about how busy things would be for at least a couple of months . . .

Much of their chatter went right over me, and I didn't mind, but I noticed when Chip asked me how I'd feel about not getting to bed until after midnight after some dinner parties, and needing to arrive no later than nine a.m. on shooting days.

I sighed, as they waited for my response.

"Okay," I said simply. "As long as I get Henry for the rest of my life, I can handle anything else."

END

Notes from the Author

Thank you for reading this second story in the Intersections Romance series.

These are short, standalone, feel-good romance novels—each with new characters and settings—but they all share the same quiet hope: that people whose bodies or minds develop outside the usual patterns can still find deep, joyful, lasting love.

The first book I finished for this series I wrote from a historically classic third-person perspective, but for *Chrysalis* I thought the main character needed a first-person point of view to delve as deeply as possible into their thoughts.

GENESIS

After finishing the first story and getting well into writing three more, I began to hope they might be good enough to make available for others to read, but selling books wasn't why I got into this.

These Intersections Romance stories began as an exercise to help me develop empathy for people with gender dysphoria, and it appears we can feel sympathy for people who are struggling without truly understanding their problems, but genuine empathy requires understanding.

"Sympathy is feeling sorry or pity for someone else's situation, often from a distance and more cognitively, without necessarily sharing their emotions. Empathy is the ability to deeply understand *and*

share another person's feelings by putting yourself in their position emotionally."

Simply reading definitions and clinical descriptions wasn't enough to help me gain empathy, but then I got the idea to write a story from the inside out—imagining myself in their places—and that helped much more.

If I understand correctly, gender dysphoria most commonly accompanies two broad experiences: being intersex (biologically both male and female to varying degrees) and being transgender (inner sense of gender that doesn't match their body's sex traits), and those two groups can overlap.

RESOURCES

If you want to learn more about being intersex, or need support, interACT can be found online at www. interactadvocates.org, and they maintain lists of support organizations around the world.

They also offer a free 3-page Patient Self-Advocacy Toolkit to support communication between intersex people and healthcare providers, especially concerning needs that many providers are not yet trained to recognize.

GRATITUDE

As always, I thank my wife Carla for her life-long support in all my many endeavors, friends who gave me encouragement with my poetry book—*Crimson Leaves: Poetry Celebrating Romance*—and the team at Wipf and Stock for their willingness to publish a novel that steps outside the usual boundaries.

BELOVED READERS

Because romance readers are human too, they also vary a great deal, and each has their own unique preferences.

If you've already read this story, I hope you found enough to enjoy to make it worthwhile, and if you jumped here first, I hope these notes have whet your appetite.

For every reader, even if there are parts you don't like, I hope you at least feel like it's *a tale well told.*

Best wishes,
John Donovan Lambert

About the Author

John Donovan Lambert

Eclectic Eccentric

Curator/Editor/Poet of
Crimson Leaves: Poetry Celebrating Romance

John and his wife Carla have been very happily married for over 40 years, with four grown children, and he was fortunate to have parents who were excellent role models and who themselves were very happily married for 37 years until parted by death.

John has multiple degrees, including history, literature in English, psychology, and sociology, which are relevant to the study of romance to greater or lesser extents, but he's spent more time independently studying romance than for all his degrees combined, in order to help him become the best husband he can be.

While studying romance in his spare time, John had a long career in I.T., until an attack of viral encephalitis knocked him into early retirement.

In the years following encephalitis, recovery has been steady but very slow, and most successful in fiction and poetic writing skills, plus the research skills necessary for writing.

In 2023 he brought back into print one of the first romance novels ever published in English, *Lindamira*, and in 2025 self-published the extensive love poetry anthology *Crimson Leaves*: *Poetry*

Celebrating Romance, which was a finalist in the 2025 Readers' Favorite Awards.

John hopes his stories of overcoming and enduring love inspire readers as much as real-life romance has inspired him.

Additional biographical information:
www.JohnDonovanLambert.com

Preview of *Toast*

Book 3 of the Intersections Romance Series

Coming Soon
Pre-Order on Amazon

The oldest, most prestigious fraternity at Ivy League Hawthorne desperately needs a contestant for the century-old, two-day cross-dressing pageant *The Toast of Hawthorne*. They choose freshman pledge Steven Maddox—the most naturally convincing candidate—but the traits that make him perfect for the Toast run deeper than anyone expects.

"Toast is both educational and deeply moving . . . Stephanie, as a character, was absolutely lovely . . . I appreciated that both Stephanie and Preston shared an abiding faith . . . What I truly loved about this book was that it is, first and foremost, a beautiful, sweet, and caring love story that, for lovers of romance and 'happy-ever-after,' will be an absolute must-read." –5 stars, Grant Leishman, Readers' Favorite

"Toast is the third book in the Intersections Romance series and continues to educate readers on different variations of intersex syndrome . . . I love that the author always includes Christian and family themes and deep lifestyle changes about intimacy, sexual orientation, and identity. The romance is mature, and seeing Stephanie find friends and love with someone who understands her and what she needs was heartwarming. The story is very engaging, with humorous moments and youthful campus vibes." –5 stars, Doreen Chombu, Readers' Favorite

"Lambert balances the comedic dialogue . . . with more serious moments . . . Lambert weaves these aspects together with a subtle Christian perspective that perceptive readers will easily recognize. Lambert deserves praise for the excellent rendition of a delicate social issue that is gradually garnering attention amongst the youth." –5 stars, Essien Asian, Readers' Favorite

EXTENDED PREVIEW OF TOAST

Pageant

Steven Maddox slowly began to wake.

He felt vaguely uncomfortable, but couldn't open his eyes yet, and struggled to get his mental bearings—without success.

After a few moments, he threw off his covers, but something felt wrong. Lying on his side, he made a very brief attempt to sit up, but collapsed with an anguished groan from a severe headache.

"Freshmen aren't allowed to drink alcohol," a voice said. "You were a very naughty boy."

He lay there, thinking . . . alcohol . . . the party at his fraternity . . . Pi Sigma Omicron. But he couldn't recall drinking. Or anything else from last night, either.

"Feel like listening?" the voice said. "We have a lot to talk about."

He exhaled sharply and forced his eyes open, which hurt, but not half as bad as moving had.

"That's it . . . back among the living now?"

"Ahhh!" he yelled as he looked toward his feet, then winced in headache pain as he grabbed at his chest.

"What the heck is this?!"

"That's the breastplate you put on last night," the other person said.

"A what?! This isn't a breastplate!"

"It is—just not the kind most people think of."

He focused his eyes in the direction of the voice—from his roommate's bed, but—it was a beautiful girl, if he wasn't hallucinating.

"I'm Annette Covington, president of the Epsilon Nu Sigma sorority."

"Ughhhh . . . w-what are you doing here? And what is this for?" he asked, poorly pulling the covers back over himself.

"I'm here to get you started on your pageant training, Pledgy. Remember?

"You promised to represent PSO in the Toast of Hawthorne Pageant, in exchange for getting out of most of the pledge initiation requirements—which is very good for you, in my opinion, because PSO has a reputation for the longest and hardest rituals among all the frats."

"I . . . I don't remember anything from last night . . . "

"They should kick you out for getting drunk under twenty-one, but I'm sure they'll overlook it this time because they're desperate . . .

"And as for what the heck that is, you're wearing a stretchy silicone breastplate with pretty realistic-moving fake boobs.

"You put it on last night and must have passed out before you took it off."

"Ughhhh . . . why the heck did I do that?"

She got her phone and started working on it.

He tried and failed to sit up again, moaning under his breath.

"Pay attention, Pledgy," she said as she hit a play button, and held it up for him to watch.

Annette turned the phone sideways and held it close to him so he could see it well while lying down.

In a crowd of raucous brothers, another new member was struggling to remove the breastplate.

That guy was standing, and seated right next to him was Steven, laughing along with everyone else.

Then when he finally got it off . . . Steven stood up to try it.

He watched himself strip off his shirt and t-shirt—and start pulling on the breastplate.

At least Steven's embarrassment was reduced a little because most of the video was blurry.

Although it took some effort, with others offering suggestions and helping tug on it—he successfully got it on.

Then he danced, swinging and swaying around to show it off as everyone catcalled and slapped him on the back to congratulate him.

And then . . . just as the video came into sharp focus, someone behind him yanked down his pants, getting his shorts at the same time, exposing him to the camera, causing him to get angry and cover himself with his hands.

"Okay, okay . . . " Steven grumbled, "so I got drunk and did something really stupid and I can be blackmailed for the rest of my life. Can you please leave me now and let me take this thing off—in private?"

"Well, first you need to know you weren't drunk when you did that, you were just caught up in the revelry and peer pressure.

"It's clear from all the videos, and every brother there will swear to that . . .

"The next thing you need to know is that when you agreed to represent PSO in the pageant, you also agreed to do everything required by the head of your training committee—that's me—and I hereby require you to keep that breastplate on until I say otherwise.

"If you take it off without my permission, you'll be breaking your promise, letting all your brothers down, and they'll kick you out of PSO."

"No!" Steven yelled, then winced again.

"No . . . !" he quietly moaned.

He struggled again and was able to sit up, and was further humiliated to see and feel the large silicone breasts swaying as he did so.

"By the way," Annette said, "they told me there was no alcohol out last night until after the main festivities, so that's how I know you weren't drunk when these videos were taken.

"The seniors—and the juniors who're over twenty-one—got out a bottle of bourbon . . . to give you your first toast, to thank you for agreeing to represent PSO in the next Toast of Hawthorne Pageant. You—"

"The what?"

"I presume one of them gave you some bourbon or you snuck a drink of it, and that's how you got drunk. With your size, it wouldn't take much.

"But I'd bet they'll all deny that they gave you any, and they'll certainly all deny that they forced you to drink any.

"And if you were to accuse them . . . you'd be expelled from the fraternity, of course, and no brother would ever help you with your career, either."

Hawthorne University in Kiawasa, New York was one of the oldest colleges in the country, and PSO was the oldest fraternity at Hawthorne, but more importantly to Steven, it was famous for having the wealthiest, most influential members.

For a business major like himself, having their friendship practically guaranteed a fast track to an executive job in a major company.

Steven sighed, his anger fading as he exhaled.

Annette saw him resign himself to the situation, and said, "You're not thinking very clearly.

"Do you think you're ready to watch the video where you agreed to be trained to compete?"

He whined, but agreed.

She queued it up and played it for him, and he watched as it started with some of the history of the Toast.

Once a year for over a hundred years, all the fraternities held a crossdressing competition, and the winning fraternity got a perpetual trophy that got passed along year after year.

The winning contestant gets the annual *The Toast of Hawthorne* trophy.

PSO had won more than any other fraternity, but hadn't won in the last eighteen years. And they *really* wanted to win again. And if they could win with a freshman . . . they'd have a shot at winning four years in a row.

Then Steven watched in astonishment as several guys had tryouts—including the breastplate—and Steven won.

He was formally presented with the offer, and to his amazement, he eagerly agreed to it all.

After that video ended he asked, "Why? I mean—why do they have such a dumb competition?"

"It started as a fundraiser," Annette explained. "They staged a *Womanless Wedding* play to sell tickets as a fundraiser, which was funny because you had big hairy men playing all the women's roles.

"At the end of the play, they had a quick vote for the prettiest 'woman.'

"They stopped doing the play a long time ago, but kept doing the competition, because . . . hey, boys will compete over anything, and this was a competition with a very long history."

"Okay . . . " Steven said, "At least I understand some of this now."

"Do you want to listen to the terms and conditions again?"

She raised her phone, but Steven said, "Just . . . tell me again.

"Slowly. And quietly."

"Okay, well, I'll give you some recent background, too.

"A big part of the contest—these days—is judged on how feminine contestants are. How they look and how they behave, in detail. Mannerisms, attitudes, sexiness, everything.

"And this year's PSO seniors must be smarter than the past eighteen years because these guys figured out that guys aren't the best people to teach a boy how to be feminine.

"Which is where my sorority comes in.

"We have a written contract—a very expensive one—to train the PSO contestant . . .

"I'm the sister in charge of your training, starting now, and I intend to win—which means I intend for *you* to win.

"And that means you not only have a lot to learn, you have to learn things so well it's second nature."

Annette didn't mention how much her sorority needed the money, and how much she wanted to bring that in for her sisters in her senior year.

"And with so little time," she went on, "I insist you stay in character twenty-four hours a day, from now until the competition.

"That means you have to keep that breastplate on as long as we say—and anything else we want you to wear. If you choose to take them off—or disobey in any way—you're breaking your pledge, and you're out of the fraternity.

"You'll be shunned."

Steven was upset at that news, but he didn't want to break his word, he didn't want to let his brothers down, and he especially didn't want to get kicked out.

But it got worse.

"So when is this pageant thing?" he asked.

"The weekend after spring break."

"Spring br—?! Are you serious?!

"You can't possibly expect me to wear this to classes! Or on my trips home! You can't seriously expect me to do that!"

"I haven't decided all the details yet, but it's seven months, Steven. And yes, they can and do expect you to keep your word regarding your training.

"You agreed to all this last night."

She started playing the video again, and he felt like his life was draining away.

And this time he paid enough attention to hear himself agree to exclusively go by the name Stephanie until after the competition was over.

He eased himself back onto the bed, dragging the covers up under his chin.

"What do you think you're doing?"

"I'm busy regretting my life."

"Well, you don't have time for that, *Stephanie*. Training starts right now.

"Your new name starts right now.

"And for your first task, after you get dressed, you're going out in public with me so I can show you a little extra incentive for you to see this all the way through."

"In public . . . ?!"

*

Verbally prodded by Annette, "Stephanie" put on her old clothes, including the loosest fitting shirt she had, which was still tight across her fake breasts.

Then they went out to Annette's sports car, which for Stephanie's middle-class background seemed like the epitome of luxury.

During the ride, Annette told her a bit about her own background.

She was a senior, majoring in finance, and although she didn't say so directly, some of the things she said clearly implied her family was very wealthy.

Still nursing her headache, Stephanie didn't say anything other than short answers to questions or polite noises to indicate she was listening.

Then Annette turned into the local Ford dealership, and drove straight to a back corner, where a car was covered by a fitted tarp.

"Okay, Steph," she said as she sent a text. "We're going to meet two guys here.

"One's the manager, and you don't need to feel embarrassed, because he knows about the competition and that the 'girl' with me is PSO's new contestant."

"That's supposed to make me feel better?" Stephanie asked.

"Yeah. C'mon."

They got out as the general manager came out and introduced himself and took the cover off the car in the corner, revealing . . .

Not a Ford, but a Porsche.

He gave the key to Annette and left them alone.

Annette handed the key to Stephanie and teased, "Okay, this may be hard for you, but pretend you're a boy, and you're going to open the passenger door for me.

"Open the door, and watch how I get in . . . because you're going to learn how to do it exactly like I do, no matter how long it takes.

"Capiche?"

"Uh, yeah, I guess."

"Oh, you're going to take a lot of work.

"An awful lot of work . . . but after you close my door, you go get behind the wheel."

Stephanie did as instructed and settled into the driver's seat.

"Comfy?"

"Yeah, of course. Does the competition include a parade or something?"

"No . . . the guys last night wanted you to agree to represent the frat—if you would—without knowing about this.

"If you win, they're going to give you this car."

Stephanie sharply exhaled and didn't say anything to that because she couldn't speak at all.

"This is a Porsche 718 Cayman GTS 4.0. It cost PSO $110,000 last year, and they're going to give it to the next contestant who wins for them.

"Their gal last year wasn't even a finalist, but that's good for you, right?

"Especially since you already agreed to everything."

Stephanie's head wasn't spinning from a hangover anymore but it started spinning now with the news of how much money her fraternity was willing to spend to win this competition—with himself as their contestant.

Annette was continuing, "PSO pays the Ford dealer here to store the car and once a week one of their people—probably the manager or their top salesperson or someone—drives the car exactly two and a half miles out and then back.

"Five miles a week, to avoid problems from sitting still too long, or something."

"You're not allowed to drive it unless you win, but you can crank it up and rev it."

Stephanie had been staring at her with a slack jaw, but finally turned her attention to the car . . .

The car that could be her car in seven months.

She caressed the steering wheel, and ran her hands over the upholstery.

Then she cranked the engine, which purred to life.

She revved the engine, then again, then harder.

"When you're done," Annette said, "we're going inside to meet the second guy. I just got a text that he's here now, and he's a lawyer.

"He also knows you're our contestant, and he's going to show you the documents and explain how his law firm is holding the car in escrow until PSO has a winning contestant.

"Then they'll transfer ownership to the winner—which *will* be you.

"Oh, and there'll be enough cash to cover the taxes on it, and the first year of insurance for you. More than enough, and anything left over is yours.

"Oh, and you're welcome to use your phone to take photos of the documents.

"And you're welcome to record the conversation when the lawyer explains things, but it seems like you're spaced out, so I'll do that for you and send you a copy.

"Okay?"

*

After the meeting with the lawyer, as Stephanie settled back into Annette's passenger seat, she said, "I'm starting to get the picture, but that doesn't explain this awful breastplate.

"This won't help me learn anything."

"Oh, but it will," Annette countered. "You can't act like a woman if you don't think like a woman—including issues with boobs . . .

"So you have to learn how it feels to be a woman . . . and learn how women are treated by men . . . and how women respond to how men treat them.

"You're even going to sleep in that or something similar, and from this moment on you're only allowed to pee sitting down.

"Those are just two of the many things we girls have to put up with that guys have no clue about."

When Stephanie didn't reply, Annette continued.

"I have five sisters on a committee with me to help me train you, and you're going to have a major crash course in what it's like to *be* a woman."

Stephanie wanted to wake up again and all this be nothing but a nightmare.

"The competition starts on a Friday evening with a ballroom event—where you'll wear an evening gown and dance a waltz with one of the guys, then a reception event, followed by a talent show.

"Saturday evening has a speech, a swimsuit pageant, and a question and answer session.

"Every frat—twenty-three of them—will have a contestant in the first three events on Friday night, and balloting will determine the top six contestants.

"Those six will compete in the last three events Saturday evening.

"Out of all six events, exactly two of your events have to be comedic, and we get to choose which ones.

"Each frat president submits a written form on Friday night with three votes.

"They'll vote for their own contestant, of course, so the real competition is for the other two votes.

"At the end on Saturday night, all the finalists will be on stage, and the celebrity emcee will hold his hand over each girl for applause.

"The loudest wins, measured by a decibel meter.

"Each frat will have twenty-five people in that audience, and seventeen frats won't have their girls in the contest by then, so those are the guys you have to get to cheer for you . . . "

Stephanie sighed.

"You look and sound bored," Annette said.

"If I tell PSO you're not making a good faith effort, they'll toss you out of the frat.

"Understand?"

Stephanie scowled, but nodded.

"Since you don't remember last night, I'll give you the rest of today to get regret out of your system, but starting tomorrow, if you aren't genuinely happy to do this, you sure better be able to act good enough to convince me you are."

Stephanie sighed again.

"Right now that seems like a very tall order," Stephanie said. "So . . . what do I have to learn?

"How to strut or something?"

"*Ooo* . . . " Annette seethed.

"You have absolutely no idea how different women are!

"You have to learn how to look like a sophisticated, sexy woman and how to behave like an elegant, congenial girlfriend.

"And to behave that way, you have to learn how to think like a woman—specifically a single woman who wants to appeal to men in every way."

Stephanie's eyes went wide with fear.

"Hey, you're not talking about me doing anything . . . freaky, are you? Like kissing a guy?

"Because there's no way I—"

"No, no, nothing like that. Well . . . no touching, but everything right up to the point of being physical.

"I've seen videos of past competitions, and studied the winners.

"The best way to win is to make those guys want you to be a real girl that they'd have a chance with."

"What?! I don't want to do that!"

"Well that's what you gave your word to do last night.

"That's what you promised your brothers . . . the ones who are counting on you to break their eighteen-year losing streak.

"And if you do, you'll not only be the toast of PSO, you'll be the Toast of Hawthorne."

Stephanie sighed.

"Well . . . give me an example of something you want me to learn. Are there any books or videos or something?"

"Oh, honey . . . you're going to learn how to shave all your body hair and keep it off . . .

"How to wear high heels, how to deport yourself—that means good feminine posture, etiquette, dancing—in the female role . . .

"How to put in and maintain hair extensions, and two major—critical—topics: fashion and makeup."

"Oh, no . . . *please* don't tell me you expect me to wear girl clothes before the contest."

"Clothes and makeup, all day, every day."

Stephanie groaned.

"And don't ever groan at me again . . .

"Your Toast committee head sent me a copy of your class schedule, and between and after classes you're going to average at least three hours a day of feminine tutoring."

Stephanie took a quick breath to protest, but drew a stern look from Annette that stopped her.

"You'll have your own room with a private bathroom in our sorority house, and—"

Again, Stephanie started to object, but stopped herself.

"You're required to keep your own bathroom clean, and it will be inspected every day and if we *ever* find the toilet lid up, or any pee that landed on the floor, it's over.

"You will have failed training . . .

"Our house only has five rooms with a private bathroom, so you're displacing one of our seniors for this.

"And that shows you how important this is to *us*.

"You'll sleep at our house Sunday through Thursday nights, and on Friday and Saturday nights you'll have your own room on the top floor of PSO."

"The top . . . the *seniors'* floor?"

"Yes. That's how much this means to them."

That made a huge impression on Stephanie, even more than the value of the car. This wasn't just something to provide them some entertainment . . . this was *really* important.

. . .

(End of Excerpt)

Pre-Order *Toast* Now
or
Add to Wishlist

www.ingramcontent.com/pod-product-compliance
Lightning Source LLC
LaVergne TN
LVHW050643100826
845148LV00011B/1961

9798385279944